Flight of Wisdom
Helen J. Anderson

The marvel of all history
Is the patience with which men and women
Submit to burdens unnecessarily laid upon them
By their governments.

~ William H. Borah.

Introduction

Andile Nklakanyno (Wisdom) Mabena often wished that he did not notice so many things. Noticing things made him unhappy. The sort of things he noticed usually concerned people and animals. He noticed when people were sad and he noticed when someone ill-treated animals or brought a puppy to the kraal and then could not feed it properly. Those things made him unhappy. He wondered why he noticed so many things that other people did not notice.

There was one particular issue with happiness and noticing things that bothered Wisdom: he was not unhappy that his mother had died when he was born. He was sorry about that but not unhappy. It did not go deep with him and he felt it should. He had never missed his mother and that made him feel guilty when he thought about it. He loved his grandmother who had looked after him since he was a baby so perhaps that was why he didn't miss his mother. When he considered the matter of mothers, Wisdom realised that many children were without their mothers even if they hadn't died because most mothers had to leave the village to earn money. He asked Ugogo[1] about his mother and she said there had never been a prettier, happier or

---

1   Grandmother

5

more wonderful daughter than his mother had been. Well that was good.

Wisdom Mabena was a child who went along with the wishes of the majority and he hardly ever took sides in an argument. He blended in with the crowd so that it seemed he did not have opinions of his own or strong convictions about anything but Mr. Mkhize, headmaster of the little school, knew otherwise.

As part of the Zulu language class, Mr. Mkhize encouraged his pupils to write essays on subjects that unbeknown to them revealed their inner selves, their fears, hopes and their lives in the kraal. In this way, he learned to know and understand his pupils.

Wisdom's writings showed that by nature he was sensitive. He also had definite ideas about life and its complexities. He had a mature and realistic outlook for his age except when it came to his naïve political views.

Wisdom believed that he would somehow be able to help change the society he had heard about. He had no experience of society other than the one he lived in so his opinions were founded entirely on the stories the villagers told when they returned on their annual leave. The society as described, the one he wanted to change, was obviously a place where no black person would choose to be.

Wisdom had heard that white people believed the brave Zulu nation were inferior human beings because they were black and had a different culture. The whites treated black people unkindly as though they had different feelings. Part of the trouble was that the whites did not speak Zulu so they did not understand the black man.

Wisdom had heard that those people who thought they were better than black people *stole land* and that was *much* worse even than people who stole cattle! The white people had stolen the black people's land.

Wisdom had never seen swimming pools or beaches but he had heard that the people who believed white was best lay in the sun at their swimming pools or at the beach for hours with *hardly any clothes on* trying to get brown! He could not understand all the things he heard about white people.

When he was seventeen, Wisdom passed standard eight. The time had come for him to decide what work he wanted to do, depending on the choices available to a black boy. He consulted Mr. Mkhize, as most of the pupils did, and told Mr. Mkhize that he wanted an indoor job, one that he could learn from but he did not know how to go about getting a job like that.

Mr. Mkhize agreed with Wisdom that he would be best suited to an indoor job and he advised Wisdom how to conduct himself at an interview. He advised him to buy a pair of black trousers, two long-sleeved white shirts and a pair of black shoes and socks so that he would be presentable at an interview for an indoor job.

Wisdom frowned in bewilderment at the impractical advice. That was all very well but where was the money coming from for such extravagance?

Mr. Mkhize told Wisdom that he would finance the initial outlay, one shirt would be a gift from him, and when Wisdom was earning a regular wage, he was to repay the loan. Wisdom was ecstatic.

Wisdom's friend, Dumisa, worked as a garden boy for a family in Maritzburg so Wisdom decided to go to Maritzburg and stay with Dumisa while he looked for a job.

Now, Dumisa was extremely worried when Wisdom arrived unexpectedly. His kaya was very small with a single bed, a shower and toilet. The law said that no visitors were allowed in his room. If the police found out, they would charge his employers and Dumisa would lose his job and then he would have to go back to the kraal. He did not know what to do because he wanted to help his friend but he did not want to lose his job.

Dumisa decided to go to Missus with his problem and ask her if Wisdom could stay as a special favour and they would be very careful. He told her that Wisdom had a pass. That was very important. He was extremely relieved when Missus said that Wisdom could stay for a few days because he knew that most employers would not have agreed. Wisdom slept on his blanket on the floor and the next day Dumisa took him to the Indian part of town for Wisdom to buy the clothing he needed to start job hunting.

Wisdom, proudly wearing his new clothes and feeling almost as confident as he looked, went to the University of Natal in Pietermaritzburg. When he arrived and saw the sprawling complex with white students everywhere, his courage deserted him. However, when he thought of Mr. Mkhize, he pulled himself together, approached one of the students and politely asked where the Personnel Department was. Mr. Mkhize had said that he should always ask for the Personnel Department. The student showed him where to go. So at least that part had gone well.

Wisdom knocked somewhat timidly on the door of Personnel and entered when asked to do so. He walked into an austere, white office with only a desk and two large cabinets in it. An efficient-looking young woman sat typing at the desk. She had a thin metal bar that stretched from ear to ear under her chin and from it there was a cord attached to a little machine on her desk. Wisdom had never seen anything like that before. He was dumbfounded and must have looked it, because she said,

"This is a Dictaphone." Of course Wisdom was none the wiser. She took the piece of equipment off her head and asked him who he was and what he wanted. Wisdom told her his name and said that he had come for a job. Without a further word, she told him to wait in the corridor. Then an extraordinary thing happened. Wisdom overheard her telephone conversation,

"This is Miss Milne. Please put me through to Professor Sinclair." Then there was a pause,

"Good morning, Professor Sinclair. Sandra Milne, Personnel, speaking." Her tone was much friendlier Wisdom thought, as though she had a smile on her face.

"I have an applicant here who seems to be the first reasonable prospect with any credentials at all to meet your requirements. Until now, the Labour Department has sent us the most unsuitable candidates. This boy may be a bit young but he speaks English and is presentable. Shall I make an appointment for you to see him?"

Wisdom knew there was a huge misunderstanding because the Labour Department had not sent him! He hoped that wouldn't spoil his chances.

Professor Sinclair came immediately and as he approached, Wisdom saw that he was much younger than he would have thought possible for a professor because he imagined that professors were old men with untidy grey hair who wore glasses, were a bit deaf and walked with a stick. Professor Sinclair walked with long strides. He had brown hair and deep blue eyes. Wisdom had never seen blue eyes before and that startled him at first. Professor Sinclair was indeed a surprise to Wisdom. Professor Sinclair asked what Wisdom's name was and when he heard it, he smiled and said, "Well, I hope you live up to your name."

"I need a right hand man, someone reliable who has common sense and who is prepared to work flexible hours. If you accept the job, you will be responsible for keeping my flat clean, doing my laundry, filing my papers, answering the telephone and taking messages when I'm not there. You would also have to attend to any other chores that might crop up unexpectedly. Do you think you are capable of that?"

"I am, Baas, I have my J.C. Certificate and I am a quick learner," he said and he proudly produced his certificate. "Junior Certificate" it stated in bold letters.

Wisdom told Dumisa that Professor Sinclair had been very impressed when he saw the certificate because he employed Wisdom on the spot. He didn't even have to *think* about it!

Wisdom could hardly believe his good luck. He had succeeded at his first interview; he had an indoor job - he was a Right Hand Man!

One

"Roger," my twelve-year-old brother, Matthew called over to me in the playground, "will you play cricket with us this afternoon? Jonathon and Steve are coming over. We're playing against Cornwall Junior next week and we want to practice."

I did not answer immediately. I knew he did not mean, "Play with us" and I was in no mood for fielding. I knew that was what they wanted me for.

"I'll make it up to you," he shouted as he came running towards me.

It usually paid off to have one of my brothers owing me a favour so I agreed.

"O.K. as long as I can stop when I've had enough." I called back to him.

I knew the whole afternoon would be a waste of time from my point of view.

My brothers were popular and had many friends mainly I suspect because we were the ones with the big garden and sporting facilities. Our Dad was an attorney a good one I think well anyway that's what people said. Far more importantly, he was a fun father with a teasing sense of humour and he was devoted to most sports. As soon as we could hold a cricket bat, he taught us the art of batting and then bowling. He installed nets in the garden and a cricket pitch to encourage us to practise and become proficient for our ages in those two aspects of the game.

We also had a swimming pool in the garden and that was considered a luxury because the beach was so close by. Dad made us responsible for keeping the pool clean and dosing it with chemicals daily so we created our own roster of duties that worked well with much bribing and bargaining between ourselves. However, there was a downside to the pool; our dad insisted that we swim a specified number of lengths, depending on our age, every morning except in the coldest months. Ten lengths became the obligatory minimum. His believed in his motto, "Healthy bodies make for healthy minds," and when Dad believed in something, he really believed in it.

Ours was a happy home though we never stopped to think about it because we took it for granted. As we grew older, our house resounded constantly with music that was too loud, stories that were hilarious and often exaggerated; outbursts of laughter and rough and tumble that could be rowdy. Then there were the wrestling matches that usually settled sibling arguments. It was a home geared to a family of boys.

I was the youngest brother and was called "*little* Roger Sinclair. I disliked the label but it stuck until I grew as tall as my brothers, a respectable six foot two inches. To be fair I think I was largely responsible for that abominable designation. When I was very young and was asked to carry out chores that I was not keen on, I would say, "but I'm too little!" and that usually worked to my advantage and later, unfortunately, to my disadvantage.

Looking back, I admire my mother for putting up good-naturedly with our noise and nonsense. She coped not only with the four of us but with our friends too who felt free to come and go as they pleased. Everyone who came to our home could count on having Mum's freshly baked scones or crumpets for afternoon tea.

From the time my brothers and I were six years old, we attended a boys' school and then at twelve we went to boarding school in Surrey, a long way from our home in Devon. The choice of schools was a topic that never arose in our family since it was a foregone conclusion that we would attend the same schools as our father had done. As soon as we were born, he had entered our names at Charterhouse. That had plunged us further into a male dominated world until we were seventeen.

I played sport at school because it was compulsory but I enjoyed the challenges of physics and science far more and in that, I was more successful.

The highlight of all activities and functions at boarding school was Speech Day when the headmaster presented the prizes and traditional speeches were made. Everyone's parents arrived for the event and that in itself was exciting. It was also "breaking up day" meaning that the long summer holiday started immediately afterwards and we would go home with our parents.

The ceremony, with our teachers dressed in their academic robes and sitting very formally in a semi-circle on the stage, held many surprises because no one knew beforehand who had won an award. The announcements were therefore a joy to some and a disappointment to others.

When my brothers won numerous cups and prizes for their sporting achievements, captain of this and captain of that, our parents displayed the appropriate delighted surprise but their pleasure was genuine. My mother usually wiped her eyes overcome by her sons' successes and my father's clapping was enough to bring the house down all on his own. I was extremely proud of my three older brothers and for my part, I was thankful that I occasionally managed academic recognition and that delighted my parents enormously. Dad usually introduced me as "the brainy one" pleased that I could do something well.

My friends and I were impatient to get on with life so we thought we would be jubilant to leave school but when the day came, we felt incredibly sad. Saying goodbye to each other, friends who had become like brothers, was a wrench and only then did we realise how close and how fond we had become not only of each other but of our teachers as well and that part surprised us.

Speaking for myself and probably for others too, when our headmaster made his inspirational farewell speech with its stirring message to us, the school-leavers, I blinked determinedly to hold back even the trace of a tear. We had always moaned that he dragged on for too long when he had something to say but to give him his due, everything he said was of value one way or another.

Pupils at our school were from different parts of the United Kingdom and some of our friends were from Commonwealth countries so by becoming members of the Old Boys Club, as we all did, we hoped to meet up again at least at annual reunions if not on other occasions.

I applied for entrance to Oxford University and from that day onwards, I watched out for the arrival of Mr. Jarvis, our Postman, whose schedule was flexible. He came at a different time each morning, depending on how many people he chatted to on the way and for how long. That made my vigil a tiresome exercise.

"You waiting for something special, Roger me lad?" he asked after the first week of witnessing my disappointment when I skimmed through the envelopes he handed me.

"Yes, I'm expecting a letter from Oxford."

"Got a sweetheart there have you?"

He took my silence as confirmation.

"Well, she'd be a right dumbbell to let you slip through her fingers – never known a nicer lad than you," he said by way of encouragement.

I decided not to enlighten Mr. Jarvis about Oxford. He had been our neighbourhood Postman for many years and he was the source of local gossip; never malicious it must be said but I did not want him to circulate my rejection if it happened.

My nerves failed me when he finally delivered the long awaited, Oxford stamped envelope addressed to Mr. R.J. Sinclair.

I almost wished it hadn't come so that I could go on living in hope but it had come and I had to open it. I took a deep breath, took my penknife out of my pocket and then slit the side of the envelope with the same precision and reluctance that one feels when preparing to swallow a vile-tasting medicine and then having decided to take the plunge, did so with great haste in order to get it over and done with.

My eyes scanned the words with a measure of anxiety and then in my excitement, I shouted out aloud, "I've been accepted!" Mr. Jarvis was hanging around so I told him the good news.

"I'm glad that's all it is," he said somewhat deflated, "I thought a lassie was stringing you along. Oh well, I'll be off now. Good day to you lad." He sighed, adjusted his postbag and went on his way.

I held the letter reverentially, mesmerised by the words, and hardly heard what Mr. Jarvis said.

"Thank you for the post Mr. Jarvis," I called after him.

Our family celebrated by going out to dinner that night, dinner that included champagne and that happened only on very special occasions.

Two

*U*niversity proved to be a painless transition from teenager to adult. I met and associated with women for the first time and slowly managed to overcome my social inadequacy in their company. Apart from the academic learning I enjoyed, I was grateful for the opportunity to meet people from different backgrounds and nationalities, of experiencing the uniqueness of English pubs and the pleasure of rowing on the river. It was a carefree time.

My first girlfriend, Vanessa, was tall, willowy and musical. She played the harp with grace and brilliance and I basked in reflected glory being the envy of many of my fellow students and no doubt of other men too. One evening as Vanessa and I strolled along the banks of the river as we usually did in the evenings and holding hands as we always did, she asked me if I would sign up for ballroom dancing lessons with her.

"A new dancing school has opened and we could start with the first group," she said enthusiastically. "We are the ideal height for each other and should make a good couple in that too." She smiled into my face and my heart melted as it always did when she smiled that way as though no one else in the world existed for her. There was no way I could deny any reasonable request that Vanessa made of me.

"I've never done anything musical in my life so if you make allowances for that, then I'm all for it."

"As long as you can feel the music, you will do well and bear in mind, we will all be beginners." She did a little pirouette in front of me and then laughed disarmingly. It crossed my mind not for the first time that Vanessa was the most uncomplicated and the happiest person I knew. She seemed to skim along the surface of life and noticed only the good things that happened as though there was nothing unpleasant in the world, at least not in hers.

So that was settled. I hoped I would be able to *feel* the music!

Everything went well for the first few lessons and then whenever the teacher, an Italian named Valerio, needed to demonstrate a new step he asked Vanessa to partner him. She was delighted to be singled out for the honour of dancing with the maestro. He twirled her around in a grand display of dancing professionalism and I noticed with a good measure of jealousy, justified under the circumstances, that she smiled down into his face in exactly the same way as she smiled into mine. Would Vanessa consider them the ideal height for each other I wondered with a sense of smug satisfaction, she was a head taller than Valerio!

Alas, I was no match for the Italian's dancing expertise nor his Latin good looks, that is if you liked those looks which I certainly did not, so I lost my girlfriend and with that my envied status as Vanessa's boyfriend. Jenny, a plump, fun-loving soul, rescued me from humiliation and with much amusement; we sashayed our way through the lessons managing to complete the course without any proven ability.

My broken heart mended surprisingly quickly and I was quite relieved the way things turned out because I was able to join in with student life again. Vanessa had been very possessive of my free time.

After graduating from university, I accepted a part-time job in the field of research as well as the position of resident lecturer for two days a week at the university. Both enabled me to work towards my PhD. During that period, I received an invitation to attend a congress of physicists in Delhi, India, at which there were to be international delegates from countries including the United States, Australia and Europe. I had never been beyond the borders of the British Isles, so I looked forward to the experience with pleasurable anticipation. To take full advantage of the opportunity, I went to Delhi a couple of days before the congress began so that I could gain an impression of the surroundings and the people living there.

My first impression of the city and therefore of India too was that it was a fascinating, extraordinary place where traffic was chaotic and of necessity, slow moving. Drivers seemed to take their hands off the hooters only long enough to change gear while pedestrians took no notice of the bedlam and walked nonchalantly over the wide roads. Rickshaw pullers added to the traffic hazards as did the cattle that lay where it suited them and chauffeurs, even of large trucks, managed to circumnavigate their way around the beasts. Mothers carrying babies with deformed limbs zigzagged their way through the traffic begging for a few coins from the drivers of vehicles they approached. The most extraordinary sight was that of dozens of scooters, each built to carry one passenger and many of them carrying a family, father, mother and a child. So much for the traffic and its hazards, I had never seen anything like it.

The city appeared to be unpolluted despite the hectic activity on the streets and the sky was clear and blue. Shrubs, tropical plants and trees, particularly the scarlet flame-of-the-forest, were as colourful as the peasants who went about their activities in the confusion of their environment. The sun shone warmly and I was glad of that having come straight from a cold English spring.

The congress was late in starting mainly due to the shambles at Delhi airport; hundreds of people, lost luggage, slow Immigration and Customs clearances not to mention the chaos caused by frantic people not knowing their way around and not finding anyone they could ask. Delegates to the congress were no exception when it came to unforeseen delays.

I was one of the first to register and went downstairs to read an English newspaper while I awaited the belated start of proceedings. There was nothing of particular interest in the paper but with nothing else to do, I knew I would read it from the first page to the last. I glanced up from time to time to see what was going on around me but there was nothing happening until quite by chance I caught sight of the most gorgeous young woman I had ever seen and she was walking towards me!

"Excuse me. Do you by any chance know where registration is taking place for the Physics Congress?"

"Yes I do." I answered, "I'm one of the delegates, Roger Sinclair. Registration is taking place on the first floor but be prepared to join a long queue because few people have managed to arrive in time."

"Thank you. My name is Alysha Patel. I'm from South Africa." Her smile was dazzling. "I'm late due to problems at the airport."

"Miss Patel, may I say that you are wearing the most beautiful sari I have ever seen?" What I really meant was that she was the most beautiful woman I had ever seen.

"Thank you, and now I had better go upstairs to join the queue."

Whew! I had to catch my breath.

There were two women on the course, Alysha and an older woman, Molly from Denver. I managed to sit next to Alysha at dinner that night and for most dinners for the entire week. In retrospect, that was not difficult because the majority of men appeared to feel slight resentment that there were any women delegates at all. Men were inclined to regard Physics as their sole domain and perhaps before meeting Alysha I may have been of the same mind.

Most young women of my acquaintance had few career ambitions of their own because society and particularly their mothers, expected them to find suitable husbands, to settle down to domestic bliss and produce families of whom everyone would be inordinately proud. The women who went to university usually studied languages or the arts and that gave them the opportunity to meet men of intelligence with good prospects for the future. They were not too concerned about what they themselves would do with their studies. At least, that was the impression we male students had.

At dinner one evening, I mentioned that I was considering making a trip to the Taj Mahal when the congress ended. A few delegates had been there and others couldn't spare the time to go. I asked those who had been what transport they had used to get there.

"Would you like me to go with you? Alysha asked from across the table, "I've been there before and would love to see it again."

"I cannot think of anything better."

The hours I spent with Alysha seemed to take precedence over the importance of the congress. However, that was not entirely true because it was in fact a most fascinating and informative experience with top class international speakers.

It was inspiring to hear of the new developments in our field. Development work was not only taking place at great pace in the United States, but in Russia too. That was a closed book to the outside world because everything that went on behind the Iron Curtain was secretive and therefore perceived to be sinister and dangerous. The two countries, Russia and the United States, were engaged in a desperate race not only to keep up with each other but also to surpass the other in knowledge and achievements.

I admired the American delegates not only for their slick presentations but also for the fact that in the beginning they were the ones who did all the talking. They were brimful of confidence, vied for the limelight and they were keen public speakers. As the week progressed, I still admired those qualities but we, the Europeans, recognized that their knowledge was no greater than ours. Due perhaps to their training from schooldays onwards they felt it imperative that in order to make an impact, they should be seen and heard. It was probably considered the best way to stand out in a crowd. The differences between us were cultural but ultimately that was unimportant because we all got on well together and we learned from each other.

When the congress ended, I asked Alysha whether we should leave after breakfast the next morning on our trip to the Taj Mahal or should we wait until after the rush hour.

"Rush hour? Its always shambolic whatever the time of day." she laughed. We left after breakfast.

We travelled by taxi from Delhi to Agra, a distance of 250 miles. It was a hair-raising journey. The drivers of vehicles, cars, trucks and buses, seemed to be fatalistic with no respect for the rules of the road, if there were any. We were appalled at the number of accidents we passed along the way. Overturned buses were left abandoned at the side of the road as were burned-out cars. Pedestrians and cyclists took their lives in their hands as they tried to cross the road or simply to get from one point to another on their own side of the road. The drivers neither slowed down nor stopped for anyone or anything. I dared not look when at times there were children playing at the side of the road.

I thought we should have gone by train – until I saw one! There were hundreds of people packed on the roof creating a very colourful scene but no doubt an extremely dangerous one. Perhaps the train was built for that purpose with a safety rail to prevent people from falling over the side, but that could not be seen from a distance. Regardless of the safety factor, how the train managed to move at all with such an overload was a mystery and it looked to be travelling at a reasonable speed.

Despite the risks on the roads, the miles and the hours seemed to fly by - such is the illusion of time when one is content with the present. I was certainly content sitting next to Alysha; I had never felt happier. Judged by travel standards in England, we had taken an extraordinarily long time to reach our destination.

My first view of the Taj Mahal was unforgettable. I had seen many photographs and illustrations of the monument so it was a familiar sight and probably for the very reason that it was so familiar, seeing it in reality filled me with breathless wonder. I would never have forgotten that moment whatever the circumstances but being with Alysha, every detail of my first impressions would remain fresh in my memory forever. I knew for sure on that day that I was not only attracted to Alysha, I was madly in love with her. It was too soon to make any such declaration and besides she may well have had a fiancé at home. I knew she was not married. Together we admired the spectacular view of the famous white marble mausoleum, and then we went inside.

One of the most striking impressions of the Taj Mahal apart from the building itself, was the total lack of commercialism. There were no junk shops with cheap souvenirs in the vicinity and no gaudy advertising. The unspoilt surroundings had not changed throughout the centuries and the people living in close proximity to the Taj Mahal continued to live a simple life in much the same way as they had always done. Their homes were basic by any standards and they used paraffin lamps for lighting.

We managed to get two rooms at a nearby hotel so we decided to spend the night in Agra and treat ourselves to more sightseeing the next morning. Could it get any better I asked myself!

Alysha was excited showing me everything that she knew so well. Her enthusiasm was infectious and I was enjoying every moment as she related the interesting history, much of it romantic, of other famous buildings in the area.

On our long and equally hair-raising journey back to Delhi, I asked Alysha about Apartheid in her country.

"It is a contemptible system in which the entire black African population are the most oppressed victims. They are long-suffering but I fear the day when their patience will run out. Tens of thousands of Indians too live in poverty in places like Cato Manor and Chatsworth and their lives are very tough."

"Poverty exists to a certain extent in all countries but are Indians discriminated against in the same way as Africans are?"

"We are all discriminated against!" Alysha sounded as though it was an effort to control her anger so I regretted asking the question.

"We, the fortunate affluent Indians, have a decent life with our own comfortable homes, good cars, cinemas and an Indian university nearby. We own some of the most valuable commercial property in the centre of Durban. In spite of that and having to pay high taxes, quite apart from being well educated, we do not have the franchise. Not only are we precluded from voting, we do not enjoy freedom of movement. For example, the authorities do not allow us to travel through the Orange Free State, one of our provinces, without official permission to do so and we have to be out of there before dark! The Orange Free State you see is the hotbed of Afrikaner nationalism."

"I can hardly believe it."

"That doesn't surprise me because our government's propaganda machine paints a very different picture of apartheid for the benefit of the international community. Very few people overseas are well informed."

"You live near Durban, a city that I believe is English speaking. Are the English as narrow-minded as Afrikaans speaking people?"

"There is no way of knowing what people feel but everyone is bound by the rules and regulations of Apartheid."

"Is Durban a pleasant city?"

"Durban is a beautiful tropical paradise, an exceptional city with lovely beaches. There the pace of life is slower than anywhere else in the country mainly due to the hot and humid climate that is responsible for our attitude, 'What cannot be done today, can be done tomorrow.' The rest of the country refers to it as Natal Fever. On that positive note, I would rather change the subject of my country and of the abhorrent government that rules it if you don't mind." Alysha was obviously irritated. I hoped more with the topic under discussion than with me for introducing it. I didn't know her well enough to judge.

"We'll change the subject right this very minute. We are having far too good a time, as long as you keep your eyes shut to what is going on in the streets and around us, to talk about unhappy situations! This traffic is something else."

Alysha's mood had changed. She was quiet and withdrawn so I did not attempt to find any other area of discussion. She managed to snap out of it, appeared to have put thoughts of apartheid out of her mind and for the rest of our journey, our conversation was light-hearted and of unimportant content.

I invited Alysha to visit me in Oxford before returning to South Africa saying that I thought she would find the university city most interesting. I had an ulterior motive of course; I could hardly bear the thought of saying goodbye to her and I hoped in this way to delay her departure for a few more days. Unfortunately, she had pressing commitments and had to go back to South Africa that same week so we agreed to write to each other.

Alysha's flight left before mine so I was able to see her off before going to my departure lounge. Our parting was painful, at least for me. I hugged her and whispered that I loved her and she smiled in a Mona Lisa sort way, a smile whose meaning I couldn't read. She did not comment but our kiss when we said goodbye was lingering and that gave me hope for the unknown, unpredictable future. We had hardly said goodbye and I was already longing to see her again.

Once back at Oxford, I awaited her letters with eager anticipation and hers, like mine, were frequent and affectionate.

Two years passed and during that time, Alysha and I made tentative plans to see each other but somehow those plans always fell through. I wanted to visit her but she said that would be awkward because she could not invite me to stay with her family and we would not be free to socialise. She wrote of her work, of her family, the book she was currently enjoying, the films she had seen and how fondly she remembered the perfect week in Delhi and our memorable trip to Agra. Judging by the tone of her letters, I didn't think that there was any other man in her life. There was certainly no other woman in mine.

Whenever I met an attractive, eligible woman, I invited her out but nothing serious developed because Alysha was always at the back of my mind and I wondered rather despondently at times, whether I would ever be able to forget her. Consequently, my life lacked prospects in the field of romance, love and marriage but I accepted that philosophically and enjoyed bachelor life as best I possibly could. I often went to London because it had never lost its magnetic charm and in that wonderful city, I soaked up culture, museums, galleries, shows and I looked up friends. Many of my friends were married and I was beginning to find the adorable little darlings they had produced, at first charming and then distinctly tiresome as they grew older. 'Uncle Roger' indulged the kids with gifts and then beat a hasty retreat when they became fractious.

One gloomy, grey day at the end of a disappointing English summer, I watched the driving rain as it lashed against the windowpanes. I had planned to go to the library but changed my mind and instead I settled myself comfortably to read the latest scientific journal. I had only just opened the paper when an advertisement caught my eye, "The Education Department of the Government of South Africa, requires the services of a Senior Lecturer of Physics for a contract period of two years."

I stared at the headline while tantalizing thoughts raced through my mind. What an opportunity! The idea of seeing Alysha again filled me with excitement and longing; she epitomised for me all that was desirable in a woman, someone with whom no other woman could compare. Had she really been as feminine, as beautiful, charming, intelligent, kind and gentle as I remembered her? Was it possible that she, or any woman, could possibly be all those things?

I decided to make a cup of coffee and to sit quietly for a few minutes to prevent exciting ideas from running away with me, to prevent myself from acting too impulsively. I looked at the window again, at the steady rain and I considered the wonderful climate that was one of the many advantages to life in South Africa. I had made up my mind! Without further hesitation, I applied for the job.

Within ten days of submitting my application, I received a phone call to arrange an interview in London. Shortly afterwards I was offered the position in South Africa at a surprisingly good salary though the financial aspect played no part in my decision. I was ready to go!

The contract was generous and flexible within certain limits and it allowed me to choose in which university town I would live since my work would entail lecturing at a number of universities at specified intervals. From the choices made available to me, I opted for Pietermaritzburg because it would be the nearest to Alysha. I wrote telling her of my movements and when I did not receive a reply before leaving, I put it down to delays in the postal service.

I had not had a holiday or been out of England since India so I decided to make the most of my journey to South Africa. I booked a passage on a Union Castle boat, the Pretoria Castle, and wrote telling Alysha of my plans and the date on which my boat would sail into Durban harbour.

The voyage was everything I had hoped it would be, relaxing and fun and I met many South Africans. They were mainly young people who were returning from Europe after a-once-in-a-lifetime trip and I soon learned that "going overseas" was the thing to do particularly for girls.

The cruise, Southampton to Cape Town, took two weeks. The weather was perfect. Temperatures were warm and we, the passengers and crew, lived in our own compact little world that sailed serenely across the ocean. Occasionally dolphins leapt out of the water and swam parallel to us seeming to enjoy the proximity of our boat.

I played bridge most afternoons with three other men, two South Africans and a Canadian. One of the South Africans, Graham, was a strapping, suntanned, outdoor man, a game ranger in the Kruger National Park. From the moment his Swedish wife Magda stepped on board the passengers were mesmerized by her. She was a Nordic beauty, tall and blonde. When she spoke and that was not very often she sounded like Ingrid Bergman. That added to her fascination and men fell over themselves for her. Magda spent her days at the swimming pool wearing a different scanty bikini every day. Stretched out on a deckchair, she displayed long and shapely legs. Many male passengers found reason if not to swim or sunbathe, then at least to walk past the pool a number of times a day. Some took up jogging that they had never done before and that entailed a few rounds on the deck before plunging into the pool.

Graham seemed indifferent to the extraordinary interest his wife generated and apart from checking up on her now and again, they spent little time together. Perhaps for that reason rumour had it in our small world of the Pretoria Castle, that they were not a suited or happy couple. Everyone had an opinion about Magda. Most men thought Graham was a lucky bastard and told him so. The women had other ideas the consensus being that she had a figure 'to die for' but they wouldn't trust her as far as they could throw her. Happily married or not, it was difficult to visualise Magda in the role of a game ranger's wife.

Len, the other South African was the best bridge player with whom I had ever had the pleasure of playing. He had travelled the world and he found that no country could compare in any way with South Africa.

"Travelling makes you appreciate home," he said.

He told us that he had financed his travels from the proceeds of six months on a whaler in Iceland when he was twenty. The money he saved during those months, he had invested exclusively for travel purposes. Iceland he said was a country of great scenic beauty.

"I earned extremely well but it was hard labour, gory work, no comforts and very tough company. I saw life in the raw and living for months with men of that ilk, you could not afford to fall out with anyone. Made a man of me," he added without a hint of bragging but as an irrefutable fact of which only he could be the judge.

Then there was Geoff my bridge partner, the Canadian. He was a quietly spoken professional golf instructor who hoped to make a better living in a year-round sunny climate than he had been able to do in Toronto. His wife would join him when he was settled and had a steady income.

Those bridge sessions were so enjoyable that seldom was one of us late in sitting down to deal the first hand of cards. Our discussions in the bar afterwards were absorbing and were far removed from the merits of Goren, Acol, conventions or transfer bids.

A band played dance music every evening and dancing on the deck was a romantic experience or would have been for me had Alysha been there. A number of love affairs started during our voyage and I wondered how many survived those idyllic days and romantic evenings on board when confronted later with normal everyday circumstances.

When the two leisurely weeks ended, a farewell party on the eve of our arrival in Cape Town was a festive celebration with excited passengers exchanging addresses and promises to keep in touch and maybe some did. At the end of the voyage, most of us radiated well-being and golden tans so different from the pale version of ourselves that had sailed from Southampton only fourteen days before.

Three

*T*he Pretoria Castle docked in Cape Town harbour early in the morning. Table Mountain as it came into view was a splendid sight, one worth getting up at daybreak to experience as many of us did. The scene of the famous mountain at sunrise with a sleeping city nestled at its base, caused emotional reactions from returning South Africans and brought tears to the eyes of many. Cape Town was a charming city but I was eager to get to Durban and that took another few days once we sailed from Cape Town.

The last days of the voyage seemed never ending stopping as we did for a day in Port Elizabeth and East London. In my impatience, I regretted not having flown from Cape Town to Durban. Finally, we arrived at my longed-for destination. Sailing into Durban harbour was the most exciting few hours of the whole journey for me and I felt my heart quicken with eager anticipation.

There had not been a black face on board so I suppose I should not have been so surprised that when the boat tied up at the quay and there were hundreds of excited people waiting to meet friends and relatives, there was not one black face amongst them. The only black people in evidence were labourers. That was my first experience of apartheid though I did not recognise it for what it was at the time.

I soon realised with a sinking heart and devastating disappointment, that Alysha had not come to meet me. She must have had some very good reason for not being there so I wrote a quick letter giving her my address. I phoned her as soon as I arrived in Maritzburg and several times after that but she was never available and she did not return a single call.

After a fortnight had passed, it became obvious that Alysha was not going to contact me, not by letter nor by phone so I concluded that she must have met someone else and was at a loss to know how best to break the news to me. Surely, she could have been honest with me. After all, she had never said nor written that she loved me so it was not as though she would be betraying me if she preferred someone else. I could hardly bear the cruelty of my dashed hopes and expectations.

In spite of my crushing disillusionment, I settled down quickly to life in Maritzburg with its peaceful, colonial atmosphere. Although small by U.K. standards, it was one of the best-preserved Victorian cities in the world, the last outpost of the British Empire.

My first day of lecturing at the start of the new term, quickly revealed that I had a challenging job on my hands. I had expected more of the academic standard of the students, all white, and hoped therefore that my services would indeed be valuable. Success would depend entirely on the students doing a tremendous amount of groundwork before they could benefit from my lectures.

At lunchtime on that first day, I went to the canteen that was crowded with students. The din of cheerful conversation and laughter was deafening. I looked around me to see if there was a spare table anywhere and noticed someone beckoning to me from the far end of the room. Relieved, I walked over to him and he introduced himself,

"I'm Nigel Buchanan and you must be the new Physics lecturer, Roger Sinclair, from Oxford," he said putting out his hand to shake mine and then without waiting for a reply, he introduced me to the other staff members at the table. They were a friendly group of people who went out of their way to welcome me into their midst. Before the meal ended, Nigel invited me to his home,

"You probably don't know anyone in Maritzburg. Would you like to come to my house for a braai and a swim on Sunday, very informal of course? My wife Elaine loves meeting people from England so we will both be delighted if you join us."

"Thanks a ton but what is a braai?" I asked.

"A barbecue."

Nigel scribbled his address and telephone number on a scrap of paper. That was how our friendship began.

On first meeting Elaine that Sunday morning, I was surprised at how alike she and Nigel were. Had I not known better, I might have taken them for brother and sister. They were the same age, same height, both were extraverts and both had dark brown hair and twinkling eyes. There was never a dull moment in their bright and breezy company. Over the course of time, they included me in many of their social activities particularly their superb dinner parties at each one of which there was an eligible woman present. I appreciated their hospitality particularly as there was a twenty-year age difference between us. I was thirty.

Nigel and Elaine were the first people to introduce me to the complexities of the social system in South Africa that they accepted at face value and expected that everyone else did so too.

Nigel was enormously proud of his South African roots.

"My great grandparents on my father's side arrived in South Africa with the 1820 settlers and my maternal grandparents arrived in 1885 from Scotland so I am a South African through and through," he told me proudly.

Elaine's genealogy in South Africa did not go back quite that far and although she was a strongly patriotic South African, she loved everything about England, having visited there twice.

"I admire the Royal Family," she told me "You have no idea how exciting it was when the King and Queen visited South Africa with the two princesses in 1947. Then there was the romantic marriage between Princess Elizabeth and Prince Philip. I had never seen such a gorgeous couple. He was so handsome. But now … what do you think of his dalliances?"

"I have no opinion because I didn't know that Prince Philip played around," I answered in all honesty.

Elaine was more 'British than the British' to quote what was often said of Natal people. She then asked me about the Queen's private life and of Prince Charles romances.

"Sorry, I am hardly a good source of information on the subject. I don't move in Royal circles and I must admit to not reading gossip magazines so I think you know much more about the royals than I do!" She was clearly disappointed.

Despite her rather loose but clearly cherished ties with England, it soon became evident that Elaine, and Nigel too for that matter, could not tolerate anything that reeked of disapproval of the South African way of life. Even if nothing disparaging was intended, they were hypersensitive to supposed criticism in any form particularly when it came to the apartheid issue. There was so much to admire in the county so I concentrated on those attributes and tried not to let politics creep into our discussions. That was no easy feat since it seemed to be everyone's favourite topic and everyone agreed with everyone else.

Another couple who did their best to make me feel at home was Sally and Jeremy Thompson. Sally was the secretary to one of the professors at the university and was a popular member of staff. She was a bouncy little person, auburn-haired, full of vitality and good intentions.

During a tea break between lectures, Sally invited me to the Pietermaritzburg Country Club,

"We live in a flat without a garden so we always entertain our friends at the club. Would you like to join us for brunch on Sunday?" she asked.

I accepted her invitation and it transpired that Sally was on the committee at the club and both she and Jeremy were "passionate about golf and Jeremy has a handicap of eleven" of which they were both extraordinarily proud.

Jeremy, I discovered when I met him, was a financial adviser and he was involved in local politics with ambitions to fulfil a significant function in the national opposition party, The United Party. He was a serious person not much given to light-hearted discussion as I soon found out, so it was not surprising that on our first meeting he put me in the picture regarding an interesting educational fact of which I should be aware he said. It was the strict separation of the English and Afrikaans sections of the white community.

"There is no love lost between us. It all goes back to the Boer War you see."

"I can go along with the fact that there's no love lost between you but what do you mean by 'strict separation'?"

"Well, it is not only a natural division between the two white groups who feel historical antipathy towards each other but it is also legislated by law. The law does not permit English-speaking and Afrikaans-speaking children to attend the same schools and universities so that each language group has its own educational institutions. No exceptions are made although there is leniency at private schools that do not rely on government subsidies".

"I gather from what you say then that segregation is not restricted to race but to a lesser degree, it applies officially to the two language groups of the white community."

"That's right and it works well. Marriage between people from the two different language groups is not fully accepted and neither of their families welcomes it."

I had recently learned that Chinese people were classified "non whites" while Japanese were classified "honorary whites," the latter because of trade relations between the two countries. The complicated structure of discrimination in South African society was mind boggling. What outsider could ever know these things! The most surprising part was that everyone, or at least every white person I came in contact with, accepted the status quo without question.

Jeremy made no secret of the fact that it was a great disappointment to them that they had no children,

"Sally wanted to adopt but we decided not to go down that road because so many characteristics both mental and physical are genetic and we wouldn't be up to dealing with difficult problems of that nature." He sounded defensive so I assured him that he was right to consider all aspects. I wondered how Sally felt in the matter because it was obvious that she was in awe of her clever husband and she agreed with everything he said.

Sally sponsored my membership of the club and I became an associate member due to my temporary status in the country.

I soon discovered that there were splendid places to visit from Maritzburg one of them being Durban, the nearest coastal city about which Alysha had told me briefly on our journey from Agra to Delhi. It had wide beaches with wonderful surfing conditions. However, my favourite get-away was to the Drakensberg Mountains.

I usually stayed at Cathedral Peak Hotel for weekends when nothing else cropped up. The view of the mountains in their eternal magnificence filled me with joy and wonder. The scene became imprinted on my memory so that I would carry it with me forever. The exhilaration of mountain climbing renewed my energy in conditions that were superb for all levels of expertise from beginners to advanced climbers.

The peaks for advanced climbers that I particularly liked climbing were the Bell and the Outer and Inner Horns. John the Guide, a Zulu, was a true professional who knew every nook and cranny in the surrounding peaks. He was an indispensable and highly valued leader since none of us would have dared undertake the expeditions without him. John the Guide, probably in his thirties though it was difficult to judge his age, was a physically strong, athletic man and an extrovert by nature who when we reached the summit where we camped for the night told us remarkable stories. He was proud of the fact that under his guidance there had never been a fatal accident though some exciting rescues. We, and that included the South African climbers, formed a personal bond with him and on those memorable occasions skin colour did not intrude on the sense of camaraderie and the thrill of achievement that we all shared.

It was soon after Jeremy had enlightened me on the subject of the relationship between English and Afrikaans-speaking South Africans that I met a 'mixed couple.'

I was on my way to the University in Pretoria, known to everyone as Tukkies, when the car in front of me swerved so suddenly that I had to slam on my brakes to avoid it. The car spun around before the driver was miraculously able to steer it to the side of the road. I managed just as miraculously to avoid hitting his car. I stopped, asked if he was o.k. and offered my assistance. Both shaken by the incident, we shook hands and introduced ourselves; he was Boetie Pienaar.

"Just call me Boetie" he said in an accent that I could not identify at that stage,

"Everyone does."

"I'm Roger Sinclair, just call me Roger, not everyone does." He laughed at that.

Boetie was a sturdy man of above average height, about two inches shorter than I was. To look at him he might have been a rugby player. He had a cheerful face that creased readily into smiles and probably into laughter too. He had a short, neatly trimmed beard, the same reddish brown colour as his hair and he wore a safari suit as most South Africans did in their leisure time.

The cause of our near collision was immediately obvious. He had had a blow-out so I helped him change the tyre as he cursed about the condition of the roads and the unexpected objects that caused nasty accidents.

"Where are you headed to?" he asked.

"I'm on my way to Pretoria."

"Look, follow me and come to my place for grub. It's on your way."

"Thank you, I will." I answered impulsively. I suppose the invitation was equally impulsive on his part. It was actually too early for 'grub' but I was in no hurry and unexpected meetings of this sort always intrigued me and besides, I did not have to be in Pretoria before the next morning.

We set off, he driving in front of me. We travelled for many miles but as far as I was concerned, that was no problem because we were still headed direction Transvaal.

Soon after we passed the sign "Welcome to Nottingham Road," he turned off and we travelled along dirt roads. He took a sharp turn and then drove up a long driveway, an avenue of flowering jacarandas with beneath their branches, a thick carpet of blue flowers. At the end of the driveway was an Old Cape Dutch style house with a thatched roof. So this was his "place"!

Three big Alsatians came bounding from the back of the house to greet him. I was pleased they showed no interest in me because I had discovered soon after my arrival in the country that dogs were not only pets in South Africa but, more importantly, they were watchdogs and vicious at that.

His wife met us at the door. I had not expected that she would be British.

"This is my vrou Annabel," said Boetie proudly putting an arm around her shoulder. Annabel was about forty; she was of medium height and build and she had a very pretty face. She had dark brown hair, blue eyes and, surprisingly, a particularly fair English complexion despite the hot African sun.

We went inside, a cool spacious house with comfortable country-style furniture. Boetie told Annabel the story of our meeting and then he offered me a beer and Annabel a beer shandy. Annabel and I both being British, soon exchanged background information and she told me she was from Gloucestershire and had been a pupil at Cheltenham Ladies College.

"I wonder if you knew my cousin, Mary Janet Morris who was a pupil at Cheltenham Ladies." I asked her.

"Of course I did! She was Head Girl the year before I left school, someone we all looked up to. She was dux of the school in her last year. Please tell me *all* about her. What a small world!" Annabel was excited and listened with avid interest as I updated her on the trials and tribulations of Mary Janet's life.

"Soon after she left school at eighteen she fell for a handsome womaniser though she didn't know that of him at the time. He was an incorrigible cad. Besotted with him, she gave up her ambition to study genetics and married the fellow instead. They had three children in quick succession and then he deserted her for a voluptuous beauty queen. He disappeared without trace, back to Australia, so the rumour went. Mary Janet had to cope on her own without training or an income. Her family helped her financially and she was able to open a bureau assisting young people in all sorts of trouble. Then five years ago, she met a prominent business executive and another whirlwind marriage followed. Fortunately, things turned out well for her the second time around. She sold her practise, became a fulltime wife and mother with family holidays to foreign destinations every year. In fact they were in South Africa last year."

"If only I'd known she was in South Africa! It is just so *interesting* to hear this. I often think of my school friends. Living so far away, I have not been able to attend Old Girls reunions and consequently I have lost touch with my childhood companions the people I spent most of my youth with."

I had the impression that Annabel missed her old life and her friends.

About twenty minutes later, an African man wearing a chef's uniform asked Missus what time he should serve lunch. Annabel immediately invited me to stay to lunch and asked me how much time I had. She then said,

"At twelve-thirty please Samuel."

I felt at home with Boetie and Annabel and perhaps it was the combination of the hot weather, the beers and the relaxed atmosphere, that emboldened me to risk asking Boetie what his ideas were on the political situation. I said that I was a greenhorn and getting to understand the culture of the country was not as straightforward as one might think.

"It's my policy never to discuss politics but I'll make an exception for you because you are new here. I will tell you the blerrie truth about what's going on here." He was more serious than he had been since his near accident earlier in the day.

"We are ruddy crazy in this country! Let's face it. Blacks are not capable of running anything but then look at it this way, take a bunch of labourers in England, now be honest, are they be capable of running anything? Damn sure, they are not. The trouble here is that people look at the masses and sure as God, that makes them wet their pants. They are terrified of the overwhelming numbers of blacks. Instead, we should look to the well-educated individuals and believe me, there are some highly intelligent and well-educated people amongst our natives but they have no say. If they do not keep their mouths shut, they land up in the jug." He took a gulp of beer before continuing uninterrupted,

"You will soon learn that something we are helluva good at in South Africa, apart from rugby of course is prejudice. We beat the rest of the world when it comes to prejudices. No country has more of them than we have. Everyone is dead scared because of his prejudices and yet clings to them for dear life; can't do without them. I don't mind telling you, prejudice exists in my family too the same as in all others. For example, I am an Afrikaner from Benoni. Do you think my family accepts Annabel? No, they ruddy well don't because she's English. Ag, to hell with them and keep the peace I say, so we never see them. They live four hundred miles from here so that makes the rift less of a blerrie issue."

"So marrying a white person from a different language group can actually break up families?" I asked astounded at the lengths to which South Africans would go to preserve their minority cultures.

"That's right. Take me now; I cannot stomach rooineks for historical reasons and that's prejudice for you but I married one and I'm happy, I've met you and I like you. The important thing is to have an open mind and that is something that is in helluva short supply throughout the country – open minds. Stacks of prejudice but man, you have to scrape the bottom of the barrel to find open minds."

"Can you visualise that this attitude might change in the future?"

"It has to eventually. The truth is that if we don't change our bloody-minded mentality regarding the blacks and our laws dreamed up by fanatics, we are doomed to disaster. If I said this to a South African, English or Afrikaans speaking, they wouldn't call me Boetie, they would call me kaffir-boetie, intended as an insult you see. No, there's not a snowballs chance in hell of change happening while we have this government. I believe that if you have nothing to gain by rocking the boat then don't rock the boat so I keep my opinions to myself and then vote for the opposition. It doesn't help a ruddy fig but that's all we can do."

Boetie's view was a refreshing change from the way most people thought and spoke and his was an opinion that I would reflect on during my journey to Pretoria.

"Under the circumstances you mention, how do the English-speaking community accept you with the name Boetie?"

"Everyone can pronounce Boetie so why the hell should I change my name that by the way is not my real name. My name is Jacobus. I am what I am and people accept me, or they don't accept me. It's as simple as that. I have no time for hypocrites who try to be what they are not. There are plenty of those around and they are usually from bugger all anyway."

"Living here I can't imagine that you miss any other place but do you sometimes miss your hometown Benoni?"

"No, for me you can keep Benoni."

Boetie's turn of phrase amused me. He was an honest, unpretentious character and I appreciated his sincerity and his down to earth observations.

I asked about their children and Annabel brought out family photographs. They had three daughters who, having travelled on their own for the first time, were on holiday with her family in England. The girls were thirteen, eleven and nine years old.

When Samuel announced that the meal was ready, Annabel led the way to the covered veranda at the front of the house that in my opinion was the back of the house but it depended on how one regarded such an issue.

The view of the garden and swimming pool from there was one of beauty and total tranquillity. I could have sat there all day and said so.

"We love the view and usually have breakfast and lunch out here. The birdlife here is quite exceptional perhaps because of the birdbaths that we have hidden in various parts of the garden. We seldom sit out after dark because the mozzies are a nuisance in the summer and it is too cold in the winter.

"Mozzies?" I queried.

"Mosquitoes. By the way, did you enjoy the meal?"

"I certainly did. It was new to me, something different."

"We usually serve babotie when we have visitors from overseas and today we didn't even know you would be coming! It is a South African dish, of Malay origin. It's made of minced meat with curry spices topped with an egg sauce," she answered with the pride of someone who had spent hours in the kitchen – but had not. The accompaniment was avocado salad. Good grub indeed.

When I left to continue my journey to Pretoria, they waved me off with a generous I knew sincere, invitation to come back soon. Boetie and Annabel, on the face of it an ill-suited couple, were clearly a happy couple.

The rest of my journey was incident free and I arrived in Pretoria shortly before dark. It was not only a pleasant town, relatively small considering that it was the administrative capital of the country, but the mainly Afrikaans-speaking people were friendly and the students' command of English though strongly accented was excellent so I encountered no language barrier.

On my first day at Tukkies, the students told me about the Voortrekker Monument, of its significance to all Afrikaners and they advised me not to miss the opportunity of visiting the famous memorial dedicated to their courageous forefathers. The Nationalist government had built the massive structure as an eternal reminder of the Voortrekkers' bravery, of their perseverance and steadfastness in the face of all manner of hardships and dangers particularly that of defending themselves against large numbers of spear wielding attackers. In addition to the hazards they faced in their quest to settle the interior of South Africa, they endured extreme physical discomfort as they crossed the awesome Drakensberg Mountains in ox wagons.

The students, proud offspring of those early pioneers, told me that annually on the 16th December, Afrikaners from all over South Africa gathered at the monument in sacred remembrance of their revered ancestors. On that date in 1836 four hundred and eighty four Boers defeated more than ten thousand Zulu warriors. The Boers ascribed their victory not to the superiority of guns over spears but to their belief that it was God's will. Before battle began, they had prayed and vowed that if God granted them victory over the Zulus, they would commemorate that date every year.

After a week in Pretoria, I spent five days in Johannesburg lecturing at Wits and then I headed back to Maritzburg for the weekend pleased to do so because I liked Jo'burg least of all the cities. It was unappealing, unattractive and unfriendly with very little to do if you were a visitor. There were many expensive homes with beautiful gardens in the northern suburbs but the surroundings lacked character and there was no sense of community. "For me, you can keep Jo'burg!"

When I arrived back in my flat with domestic tasks to be done, I decided to take the advice of my new circle of friends who had suggested that I employ someone to do my household chores. I had procrastinated because I needed someone who could do more than household chores but I did not know how to go about finding the right person so I decided to ask the secretary in the Personnel department of the university to help me.

The secretary, Miss Milne, succeeded and within a few days, I had employed a diffident, open-faced youngster who was keen to work and keen to learn, he told me. He was young, only seventeen. The new clothes he wore had obviously come straight from a shop with the all too familiar creases in the shirt. He had a serious, almost worried expression during the interview. However, when I offered him the job, his face lit up with obvious relief and his wide smile revealed perfect, sparkling white teeth. His name inspired confidence; he was Wisdom.

Four

Wisdom was inexperienced. It was his first job and he had never been in a white man's home before so everything was new to him. He was ambitious and true to his word, he had an insatiable desire to learn and please. He seemed ill at ease with me and I began to suspect that he was unaccustomed to the company of white people. Well that made two of us; I was unaccustomed to the company of black people.

Wisdom had been working for me for about ten days when after dinner one evening, the doorbell rang. I opened the door to see him standing there looking awkward and highly embarrassed, his eyes cast down.

"What's wrong?" I asked noticing how he fidgeted.

"Nothing wrong, Sir." I had told him that I preferred not to be called "baas."

"Come in then and tell me what's on your mind."

"It's like this, Sir," he said slowly not moving from his position on the other side of the door. He paused and then seemingly plucking up courage to continue, he added at great speed and in a monotone,

"Will you buy me a flat boy's uniform?"

"What do you need that for? I'll buy you extra black trousers and shirts if you need more clothing, but why a flat-boys uniform?"

"Mdala told me that the boys working here will accept me better if I dress like them. Mdala also said that he heard the white people talking, the ones who live here in the flats, and they think I don't know my place. If they think I don't know my place they will make trouble for me so I should wear a uniform."

"What the dickens does Mdala have to do with this and who is Mdala anyway?"

"Mdala is like our father. He is old and has worked here since the flats were built."

"If that's what you want, buy yourself two uniforms."

"Thank you Sir. There is something else. I will need a pair of takkies."

"Takkies? What the dickens are takkies, Wisdom?"

"They are the shoes you see the flat-boys wearing."

"Buy yourself a pair then. How much do you need for these purchases?"

He stated an amount of money and I said he could go shopping the next day. Wisdom was obviously relieved and thanked me profusely. The next evening, he presented me with the cash slips and the change that was correct to the last cent. He looked ridiculous dressed in khaki shorts that were a size too big and ended just above his knees, a short-sleeved khaki shirt that, like the shorts, was trimmed with red. I made a point of looking at his takkies, the shoes that you see flat boys wearing, and saw that takkies were in fact what I would call tennis shoes. He told me that you could also get them in black. He beamed from ear to ear.

We had a good understanding, Wisdom and I. We were both newcomers and in our own very different ways, we both had to adjust to a new lifestyle. He had recently come from the kraal and never having been in a city before arriving in Maritzburg, the change was more radical for him than it was for me.

Wisdom lived in the servants' quarters that belonged to the flats so he was always on hand when I needed him. He was intelligent and mastered his administrative tasks remarkably quickly.

I had numerous books that had to be catalogued and put in specific order on the bookshelves and papers galore that needed careful filing. Wisdom excelled in this work, loved it and took pride in his progress. His increasing proficiency was a tremendous help and, I admitted, a welcome surprise particularly considering his inexperience in every aspect of white living standards, of modern household equipment and of clerical work. One evening when he had worked a long day, I suggested that I take him out to dinner. He looked at me as though I had taken leave of my senses.

"Do you mean to an eating place?" he asked incredulously.

"I mean to a restaurant. Get out of that uniform, put on your black trousers and get a move on. I don't know about you but I'm ravenous." Wisdom had already asked me if he could keep his black trousers, white shirts and black shoes in the empty cupboard in the spare room.

"Sir, I cannot go to a restaurant for dinner. You know about apartheid. I am black." Wisdom was brown if one had to be precise about colour. I had seen far blacker blacks in England. I shocked myself and could hardly believe that it had come down to this already. I was defining the nuances in the colour black!

He was right. How stupid of me. I had not yet arrived at the stage of knowing automatically and accepting that no social contact was permissible.

"Can we go to the township then?"

"No sir, we cannot." He was shocked at the suggestion and made a move to leave.

I told him to set two places at the kitchen table and I would get a take-away from the drive-in restaurant. I bought lasagne and when we sat down to our meal, Wisdom said he would like to learn to eat "the European way." Considering he had never used a knife and fork before, he did very well at his first attempt.

Dining together was an ideal opportunity for me to I ask him about his family and his home. He said I would not understand. "Try me." I said, and he promised to do so "some other time." I was beginning to get the hang of apartheid and the extent to which it regulated every interracial contact and I did not like what I learned of it. When occasionally I mentioned the subject at a dinner party, my remark was met either with stony silence that caused discomfit on all sides or someone would take it upon himself/herself to enlighten me as to all its advantages and that it was "so much better for everyone including the blacks." They quoted so many standard propaganda-style explanations and phrases that I gave up, never knowing whether the persons actually believed what they said or whether it was a defensive strategy employed in a highly sensitive issue.

Wisdom was my only contact with a black person and I knew nothing about him. I began to feel increasingly interested in his background, his customs and his people so one evening, I asked him to tell me about himself. He hesitated then said,

"Sir, you have never been to a kraal so you cannot understand. It is better that you do not ask." "Then we will go to your kraal!"

You could not always tell from Wisdom's reaction what he was thinking. When I said that, his face lit up with pleasure but his tone was doubtful.

"Haw!" he exclaimed slowly and then he said no more but sat in thoughtful concentration.

"Is it a good idea?" I asked hoping to discover what he was thinking.

"No, it is not a good idea because it might make trouble."

After a short discussion and weighing up the pros and cons, he agreed to my proposal and then he immediately set about making plans of which he kept me well informed.

Somehow, with messages going via, via, via different people Wisdom knew or knew of, he managed to get a message to Ugogo who would confirm with Mr. Mkhize that he would be there on Sunday two weeks later. Mr. Mkhize you see could speak English. I had not considered that aspect since Wisdom's English was very good and improved by the day.

Wisdom insisted on sitting in the back of the car "because that will be safer," he said. Safer from what I could not imagine. Wisdom could get odd ideas at times so I chose not to insist. We set off with Wisdom sitting in the back and me driving. We travelled for a few hours along the north coast road with panoramic views of the sea and were just about to cross the Tugela River into Zululand, when police officers in a police van with flashing lights, waved us over to the side of the road. As far as I knew, I had not broken any rules of the road and I had certainly not been speeding. I pulled over.

A serious looking police official with his hand on his holster came to the side of the car where Wisdom was sitting. Unsmiling, he peered in through the back window and said in a serious but not unfriendly tone of voice,

"Your pass please."

While Wisdom rummaged in his pocket, I said in amazement,

"Officer, I had no idea passports were necessary for entry into Zululand. No one has ever informed me of this regulation." He looked at me oddly.

"I'm sorry but I do not have my passport with me but if its o.k. by you I can produce my drivers licence as identification." I opened the cubby hole and took out my driver's licence."

"I must apologise for my ignorance but you see I'm new to the country." He looked at my driver's licence.

"Is this the only checkpoint between Natal and Zululand or are there others I should know of?" I asked in my assumed ignorance. He was the non-communicative type so I broke the awkward silence and volunteered added information,

"I'm on my way to visit a friend of a friend of mine. As you will have noticed, my skivvy sitting in the back isn't the brightest but he says he knows Zululand well and can get me to the address of the friend of my friend." Sitting quietly in the back, Wisdom had not uttered a word.

The police officer squinted at me sympathetically, at least as sympathetically as his expression would allow and that expression said it all – my skivvy was not the only one he'd noticed 'wasn't the brightest!'

He handed Wisdom his pass, stepped back and said with a slight trace of a   condescending smile, "Drive on." Not at all like a British Bobby I thought and immediately reminded myself of my intention not to make critical comparisons between here and there.   In fairness, the local Natal Provincial Police were polite and very different from the South African Police of which our contact that morning was a member.

When we were well out of sight of the police van, we both laughed whether because of the unnerving incident or because it really was funny, I don't know. From then on, I called Wisdom "Skivvy" except when I introduced him to people as "Wisdom my Right Hand Man."

We turned inland and drove through cane fields for another hour or two before taking a country road that was even dustier than the road through the cane fields.   Had I known what to expect, I would have hired a jeep because the potholes were appalling as was the dust that came in through invisible openings in the framework of the car. In some places, we lurched from pothole to pothole. The potholes were not the only hazard en route but - the stones! At one point there was a sign, "beware of falling stones." I wondered how anyone could possibly do that or avoid them if they tumbled down unexpectedly.

"There's been a lot of rain here. Everything is very green," Wisdom said with a measure of relief as he admired the passing scenery. "When the rains stay away, everything suffers; the cattle, the mealies and the people."

It was hard to believe with the dry, dusty conditions that we were experiencing that there had been any rain at all.

I was able to admire very little of the green countryside that he was so pleased about because I had to concentrate all my attention on keeping to the mountain road that fell away sharply on one side. We travelled up the longest, most dangerous mountain-hugging road that had ever challenged my driving ability. There was a sign that urged caution because it was "one in six." I could not imagine how that information could help anyone. It was a bit like the sign warning one to beware of falling stones.

"What happens when two buses coming from opposite directions have to pass each other?" I asked not expecting Wisdom to have any idea whatsoever. I could hardly imagine that a single bus could negotiate the hairpin bends let alone two.

"It's not busy here." He said by way of an understatement. "There are never two cars on this road at the same time. You don't pass any cars and there are very few buses. Sometimes buses go over the side, but that is never the fault of the driver. It means there was something wrong with the bus." So now, I knew. Competent drivers did not go over the side! I hoped my car would make the journey safely in both directions and that we would not meet a bus along the way.

I was surprised at my reaction to the village when we got there. I had seen pictures of a Zulu village but to see one in real life was an extraordinary experience; I was intensely conscious of being in the heart of Africa, unchanged for centuries, far from western civilisation. There were clusters of round huts with thatched roofs that constituted the kraal; there was an enclosure where the villagers kept their cattle at night. It was made of spindly tree trunks and branches held together by wire and hardly strong enough one would think to keep cattle in the enclosure if they wanted to escape. The ground was brown and hard and the view all round was of undulating hills that stretched as far as the eye could see. The atmosphere was peaceful, perhaps boring if one lived there. That was my first impression of Wisdom's kraal.

We had hardly stepped out of the car when children, mainly between three and six years of age, many of the little ones naked, came running from all directions. Our arrival must have been a highlight that broke the rhythm of their normal routine because they were excited and curious too as they observed us with smiling little faces. They made way for a middle-aged woman who too came running, her bosom bounced as she ran. She was plump and motherly; she was Wisdom's grandmother, Ugogo. Wisdom laughed when he saw her and she laughed too as she hugged him. She then stood back to admire him, and started crying. She stopped for long enough to speak to me in Zulu and then laughed. Wisdom said that she was thanking me for looking after him so well! Then she cried again.

I turned away from the intimate family reunion and guessed the laughing and crying might go on for some while yet. As I did so, a man approached me and introduced himself.

"Good morning, I'm Charles Mkhize, the schoolmaster," he said as he put out his hand.

"How do you do, I'm Roger Sinclair." His handshake was firm. I could see right away that he was an easy-going person. He wore casual, long cotton trousers and an open-neck sports shirts. He had a pleasant open face and was friendly. I could not judge his age. He may have been a few years older than I was.

"I would like to invite you to my house," he said. "I think we should leave Wisdom to his grandmother for the rest of your visit. She's been living for this day and is very excited as you can see. It's a nice walk to my house and I think you will enjoy the scenery as the countryside is particularly green after the rains we've had."

I followed Charles and as we walked along a well-trodden path with indigenous vegetation on either side, I breathed in the essence of rural Africa with its green undergrowth, expansive space and blue skies above. We passed a pathetically emaciated dog that lifted its head, barked half-heartedly using the only energy it could muster and then put its head down again between its paws.

"This dog is a sad case," Charles told me "when one of the villagers retired early because of his injuries following an accident in the mines, he brought a little mongrel puppy home with him for company because his wife had died and his sons were working in the city. He and his dog, this one, were inseparable. He fed the dog better than he fed himself. The old man lived for thirteen years after his retirement and then about a week ago while out walking with his constant companion, he dropped dead at this point probably of a heart attack. The dog is in mourning and lies here day in and day out. Despite my best efforts and those of the villagers, the poor animal has refused to eat a morsel since. It sips only enough water to stay alive. I wish there was a kind way to put it down." I agreed with him and said its death was probably imminent because it was obviously very weak. If they wanted to hasten the end, they could stop giving it water.

I enjoyed the walk as we followed one another in companionable silence. It was a treat to be immersed in the solitude of the Zululand countryside far from traffic, far from the world of ticking clocks, time schedules and commitments.

Charles's house was compact. It was built of brick and had a corrugated iron roof. I remarked that it must sound wonderful at night when the rain pelted down and he said that regardless of the type of roof, rain pelting down was always a wonderful sound to country people.

Charles pointed out the school at the base of the hill opposite his house; "Mr. Mkhize's Do Well School" that Wisdom had told me about with great pride.

I asked Charles about the school and he said that when he qualified as a teacher he had a calling to work in the Homelands to help deprived villagers.

"Zululand is a so-called Homeland but it has been split up into many parts with affluent white farming areas between our designated areas so we cannot say that Zululand as we have always known it is ours. We have bits and pieces here and there. I chose to come to this remote village where I felt I could do the most good. With the help of two dedicated women of the village, it is amazing what we have achieved for the youngsters. The children are well disciplined, happy at school and keen to learn."

We went inside and sat in his sitting room, a sparsely furnished room with three comfortable chairs, a coffee table, a desk and a bookshelf. The light streamed in giving a bright, cheerful effect. Charles made a pot of bush tea, we continued the conversation that was particularly interesting to me and then about an hour later he stood up saying,

"I'm ready for something to eat and I'm sure you must be too after your journey. I've prepared madumbies for lunch, have you ever tasted them?"

"No I have never heard of them."

"They are a root vegetable, a speciality of Zululand. I hope you will enjoy them; a great favourite of mine."

We went through to his kitchen/dining room for lunch and sat on plain wooden chairs at a scrubbed wooden table. Charles put a pot of hot madumbies in the middle of the table and showed me how to eat them. He sliced one end and then squeezed the vegetable that slithered out. A madumbi was the shape of an elongated potato but with a coarse skin and the vegetable was grey in colour. We ate them with pepper and salt.

"Charles" I asked, "would you mind telling me how apartheid affects the rural community? Does apartheid have a big influence on your lives?"

"Shall we sit outside?" he asked so I wondered whether he would answer my question.

We took the chairs outside, the ones we had been sitting on, and placed them under a spathodea tree that provided the only shade in the vicinity.

"To answer your question," he said when we were seated, "we are very privileged living here because we live without harassment.

We are able to educate the children, keep a watchful eye on their development and also pass on knowledge of our customs, beliefs and traditions. We encourage pride in the Zulu nation and in our distinguished past. The children lead a relatively carefree existence though there are always the sorrows of life, losing parents, siblings and friends to illness or disease. Country people have time for each other and they care for each other, they know no other way. However, there are two sides to the coin. We cannot prepare the youngsters for life once they leave the kraal to go to the cities. It is traumatic for their families, for all of us, when they set off to face the harsh reality of the outside world of apartheid for which they are ill-equipped. They can learn only from experience and that is a very tough lesson."

Charles looked pensive as he spoke.

"Most of the young people look forward with excitement to adventure and to the material advantages they expect of city life. With the inexorable confidence of youth, stories that filter back to the village seldom deter them and that is just as well since they have no choice but to go there for work. The girls usually seek household work and that offers certain protection but adjusting to that way of life takes its emotional toll. Some of the boys, fortunately not many, come to a sticky end and each one is a tragedy. Most of them are between fourteen and sixteen years old when they leave. We have great difficulty in coping with the heartbreak of disaster or loss when it happens."

"This is an aspect of kraal life that would never have dawned on me had I not made this visit but I can well imagine the anguish and the fear of the mothers when their sons and daughters leave the security of their simple homes to face the harsh reality of the world of apartheid. Judging by conversations I've had with people in Maritzburg, they have no idea what life is like for black citizens and I doubt they will ever know."

"Ignorance is more comfortable in these circumstances because one can live without guilt or concern for one's fellow man. People don't really want to know. We have a saying, 'Evil flourishes where good men do nothing,'" Charles reflected.

"To go back to your question; the departure of our young people to towns and cities is very worrying but the greatest tragedy of apartheid is the break-up of black family life. Men have no option but to work in towns leaving their families to manage without them. As you probably know, black families are not permitted to live together in white areas. They see each other only when the men come home on their annual leave. In fact, no one may leave the village without a pass. A pass is the single most important paper a black person can possess."

"I experienced a pass situation this morning. Wisdom and I were stopped by the police a few hours ago while on our way here. The police officer demanded to see his "It doesn't take long before law-abiding black people feel rising panic at the sight of a policeman. Our experience is that they are out to get every black man they can on some pretext or another."

"This is awful. Do women have an easier time when they go to the cities to work?"

"From the point of view of police harassment, yes they have an easier time. The women I admire the most are those who stay here to look after their families, children and grandchildren. I have the deepest respect for them and the way they manage their responsibilities and on very little money. On top of that they know their men are not faithful to them year in and year out. They just hope that their husbands will not return with venereal disease when they arrive home on their annual leave. In our culture men can have more than one wife but then only in accordance with our traditional customs. We do not believe in casual sexual affairs without commitment. The undermining of our customs and way of life is a disaster for our people. Before your visit today, I'm sure you could not have imagined an existence such as ours in which there are no men around. The lack of male influence is detrimental to the development of the children particularly the boys."

"I could not have imagined it and even now I find it hard to believe that this is a way of life imposed on your people by the laws of the land. I must say Charles that judging by the way Wisdom has turned out I think you are doing a splendid job for the children. I congratulate you. Wisdom speaks very highly of you and regards you as his surrogate father."

"I try to be that to all the children."

"Are the girls equally as interested in education as the boys are?"

"Yes every bit as much. I believe the old saying "educate the mothers and you educate the family.""

Charles and I were on an easy-going footing from the word go. He was the first black South African I had talked to about the politics of the country. In fact, he was the first African, apart from Wisdom, that I had conversed with at all.

When Charles asked me what had brought me to South Africa, I found myself confiding to him about Alysha as though it was the most natural thing in the world.

He was not shocked as others might have been and he gave me level-headed advice.

"You must accept the fact that Alysha has taken the only course open to her because a relationship between the two of you in this country is doomed to disaster. My advice is that you accept her decision that has nothing to do with whether she loves you or not, whether she has met anyone else or not; it is simply the only sensible course to follow in a country where love across the colour line is a criminal offence. You should also bear in mind that the Indians have their own culture that they have managed to preserve. It has not been devastated as our Zulu culture has been."

"I can understand the culture issue but I find it inconceivable that something as personal as marriage is legislated!"

"You will find that every aspect of life is legislated in South Africa. If, as a black South African, you read brochures advertising the delights and joys of our country, you wonder if they refer to the same country that you live in! Wonderful colour pictures of wild animals grace pamphlets and posters while no black man, apart from those who work in game reserves, has ever seen a wild animal and most whites haven't either. Those brochures illustrate as part of the attraction of our country, nubile Zulu girls wearing traditional dress, bare breasts and short, elaborately beaded skirts. Would you call that exploitation of our people and customs? Take the beaches; wonderful beaches are pictured in true-to-life colour but the signs displayed on those beaches, "For whites only" never appear on those glossy papers. No one sees the poverty, the shantytowns such as Kwa Mashu and Soweto. Tourists come to our shores for three or four weeks, gasp at the scenic beauty of the country, sing its praises and leave thinking they know all about South Africa! In my job, I never come into contact with tourists but the employees in hotels and game reserves have many amusing stories to tell about the ill informed travellers who, at the end of their two or three weeks holiday, know the country better than anyone else! In fairness that is understandable because the whites have a vested interest in what people see. He smiled wryly.

"I am grateful for the opportunity to see the situation through your eyes," I answered. "I know people who have enjoyed wonderful holidays in this country and what they mainly rave about, and quite rightly so, is the climate, the natural beauty and of course the way of life. They probably don't stop to think that there might be a different way of life from the one they enthuse about, one that is exclusive to the affluent, relatively small white community. I have much to digest from our discussion, Charles. Thank you for being so honest with me. Have you spoken to any other white man as openly as you are speaking to me now?"

"Yes, with an Irish Catholic priest who worked as a missionary not far from here. He was outspoken in his criticism of apartheid and other government policies that affect the lives and the livelihood of the blacks. That did not go down at all well with the government; 'Politics and Religion do not mix,' you see. He was deported as being a communist agitator. I have never heard from him again but that does not mean that he didn't write."

The hours passed quickly and when it was time to leave, I asked Charles whether I could come back on a future visit. His reply was disappointing but understandable.

"No, I'm sorry there's too much at stake. The police probably know you are visiting here today and they will be keeping a watchful eye on both of us. If they do not know it, and I hope they do not, then a second visit would be pushing it. They would question why an English professor should want to visit a country schoolmaster in a Homeland. You do have a lot to learn my friend. You see the only relationship tolerated between white and black in this country is that of master/servant. Anything else is forbidden. You cannot know these things but I can assure you that if you come again, we will be suspected of political conspiracy and the police will whisk me off for interrogation. I am sure you will understand that my position here is too important to the villagers, particularly to the children, for me to take chances. If the issue of race were no hindrance to our pursuing a friendship, I would welcome more visits from you. I have enjoyed our discussions. 'Uhamba Kahle' Roger and be careful."

"I am very impressed with what you are doing for the children. May I give you a donation towards school funds? "

"That is most generous of you. We have all sorts of needs so rest assured any money you donate will be spent wisely."

Wisdom and I travelled back to Maritzburg in near silence. I reflected on my conversation with Charles and hardly noticed the hazard of driving down that long treacherous road with its lethal bends in unexpected places. I had learned more from Charles about South Africans, white and black, in one afternoon than I could have learned from years of elegant dinner parties in Maritzburg.

I had achieved what I had set out to do. I had some understanding of Wisdom's background and I had learned about black people, their frustrations, their hopes and the hardship of their lives. I had also witnessed the philosophical acceptance of their circumstances that enabled them to be the happy, joyful people they appeared to be despite their adversities. The children were high-spirited and friendly.

Of course I had heard of apartheid before coming to the country, whoever had not, but I had been under the mistaken impression that it meant in essence equal but separate development of the races "who were happiest living amongst their own people and with their own traditions." Alysha had told me a different side when we had spoken of it briefly a few years before but I had not fully appreciated that in practise the tentacles of apartheid stretched wide and deep and were harsh, cruel and uncompromising.

Five

I had made up my mind to follow Charles's advice and not seek contact with Alysha. However, hardly a day went by without me thinking of her so I reasoned that if she loved me, would it not be sensible for us to discuss it and arrive at some rational solution. How could others prescribe what was best for us? If she lied to me and said she did not love me, I would see through her deceit but I would understand why she did it. If she genuinely did not love me, I would get on with my life without her but I needed definite, official closure to be able to do so. It was as simple as that. I reckoned I deserved that much having travelled six thousand miles and given up two years of my career to see her again.

Two weeks passed while I vacillated between common sense and desire and then I plunged into unfamiliar territory in bizarre circumstances if one considered that our unenviable situation arose only from the most natural thing in the world that of two people meeting and falling in love.

It was a fine Sunday morning when I set out to find Alysha's home in Reservoir Hills.

As I drove around looking for the house, it was evident that Reservoir Hills was an affluent neighbourhood with upmarket houses and country views and the sea in the distance. Reservoir

Hills was an Asian area and this I had learned was all part of the Group Areas Act. South Africans' lives were controlled probably more than any of them realised, by fear of falling foul of the law and by all the Acts. I knew some of them, the Immorality Act, the Group Areas Act, Job Reservation Act and there must have been many others I had yet to discover.

Finally, I found the house. It was a very large split-level house. The front garden was terraced and there were palm trees on either side of the driveway.

I felt apprehensive as I rang the bell and heard someone come towards it. A distinguished, middle-aged Indian gentleman opened the door. He had a kind, friendly face and black hair with streaks of grey through it. I introduced myself and before I could explain who I was, he said he knew about me and invited me into his home. He was Mr. Patel, Alysha's father.

I followed him into a formal room with carved Indian furniture much of it inlaid with ivory. I hardly noticed anything else but, at a glance, I knew there were exceptional works of art, objects and paintings.

Without any trivial preliminaries apart from introductions, Mr. Patel, a refined person in manner and speech, asked me to take a seat and he referred immediately to the congress in Delhi. He knew that his daughter and I had fallen in love but even if there were no apartheid regulations in South Africa, a marriage between people of such different cultures and religions generated many problems.

"We believe in arranged marriages. In this way, we serve the best interests of our children and our families."

"If two people fall in love, are they still bound to an arranged marriage with someone else?"

"It is not as simple as that to answer. The broad outlines are that we parents look for someone from a similar background to our own. Education is very important. If both sets of parents agree then the young people are introduced to each other. The young people are free to reject the choice in which case the search begins all over again. In an arranged marriage, love grows and lasts. Romantic love is all very well but it blinds young people to reality and it does not take into account the importance of class, family and intellectual compatibility. We believe that marriage is far too important an undertaking to be founded on something as ethereal and giddily unreasonable as romance. This does not mean that Indian women are subservient, far from it; the same conditions apply to men and women."

"How did Alysha feel about an arranged marriage before she met me?" I was very keen to hear his answer.

"She never questioned the custom but took it for granted. However, she wanted to complete her education before marrying and we agreed that that was a sensible decision. Since then, we have introduced a number of suitable candidates to her and she has turned them all down. In this she is unwise because she will soon pass the marriageable age."

"My wife and I are conservative parents and we want to see Alysha settle down to conventional family life with traditional Indian customs. She is an intelligent young woman with a good position at the Indian University. She may be able to combine family life with her career but the career alone will never bring her happiness."

I did not say a word. What could I say because I did not fit his perception of an ideal husband for his daughter? He wanted the best for her and with Indian traditions and customs so different from western ways; I could never be that.

A thoughtful silence followed.

"If Alysha should wish to marry me and live in England regardless of the complications, would you accept that, Mr. Patel?"

"You must know that even in England the middle and upper classes in British society do not genuinely accept mixed marriages. They pay lip service to it but please don't saddle them with that sort of thing in their families! You have only to look back to British India to know how the Indians were treated in their own country and what dire consequences there were for any Indians who crossed the colour line. There was one famous exception; the affair of Lady Edwina Mountbatten, wife of the last Viceroy of India, and Jawaharlal Nehru, first Prime Minister of India. Their love affair must have been a thorn in the side for the British particularly as it continued whenever Nehru visited England. By all accounts, Lord Louis Mountbatten chose to ignore his wife's infidelities."

"Mr. Patel, I appreciate your openness. I can fully understand your sentiments and your concerns regarding Alysha and me. I had not considered the cultural differences and in my ignorance, had not realised how enormous those were, or are. Thank you for inviting me into your home and for taking the time to enlighten me in the kindest possible way. I'll leave now." I put my hand out to shake his.

"Don't be in such a hurry. My wife will never forgive me if she doesn't meet the man who stole our daughter's heart. Apart from that, we will not let you leave without giving you some form of refreshment. What can I offer you tea or something stronger?"

I glanced at my watch and noted that it was almost twelve o'clock. Twelve o'clock was sacred when it came to daytime drinking in South Africa, not before twelve o'clock! I said I would have a beer.

He left the room. A young woman came in, greeted me politely and put a tray of drinks, glasses and snacks on the table in front of me and then she left the room.

Mr. Patel returned with his wife. I saw immediately that she was Alysha's mother. Alysha had inherited her mother's beauty. They had the same slender figures and walked with the same feminine grace, a likeness that was barely credible.

Mr. Patel introduced me to his wife who spoke with the same eloquence as Alysha did.

"I am pleased to meet you Mr. Sinclair. Welcome to our home. You have been in South Africa for some weeks I believe. What are your thoughts on our country?"

"The country is beautiful and the weather is wonderful; I am sure all visitors say that. If apartheid did not exist, South Africa would be a paradise but unfortunately, apartheid does exist."

A short discussion on the subject followed and then about half an hour later, I said I would be on my way and I thanked them for their hospitality.

Mrs. Patel took my hand in both of hers and said,

"You have gone to great lengths to see Alysha. We appreciate your efforts to meet our daughter again but under the circumstances outlined to you by my husband, you must see how impossible a marriage is between the two of you."

"Yes, Mrs. Patel, I do understand the complications and I have accepted the situation, very reluctantly I might add."

"If Alysha agrees to see you now, how would you feel about that?"

"*How would I feel about that?* If Alysha wants to see me, then with your permission, nothing in the world will drag me away before we see each other again."

Without another word, she left the room and Mr. Patel and I waited in silence. I watched the door not knowing whether she would come through it or not and if she did, how would I feel seeing her for the first time in two years and in the presence of her parents. How would she feel? Had she changed in the meantime? Had I changed? My heartbeat quickened.

Then there she was!

We looked at each other and I saw a vision of loveliness in an exquisite, graceful sari. I was bewitched by the same magic that had enthralled me two years before. As Alysha entered the room, the thought flashed through my mind that a sari must be the sexiest dress ever created. It was modest and feminine and yet, tantalisingly, it revealed a bare midriff and a slim figure that was shown off to perfection.

I never knew how it happened but we were instantly in each other arms. We did not kiss but we hugged each other with the desperation of two people about to lose what was most precious to them. Time stood still and I wanted it to stay that way. We were alone in the world oblivious of all else. Then I held her at arms length so that I could look at her face, into her eyes and at her mouth that I longed to kiss. Neither of us said a word.

I cannot recall how long it was before we became aware of our surroundings of not being alone. Alysha's father coughed discretely possibly embarrassed at the scene before him. I then kissed her and my dream of marrying her, goodbye. I realised that the time had come for me to accept the inevitable. I would not be the first man and nor the last on whom love or circumstance had played a dirty trick.

I decided to utilise the rest of my contract period not only in lecturing, reading research material and trying to forget Alysha but also in seeing as much of the country as I possibly could before returning to England.

My future did not lie in South Africa. I knew that. I could not stand the political climate, I had nothing in common with the mentality of South Africans and I had to think of my future as a scientist. I knew too that I would never regret my South African adventure during which I had learned and no doubt would continue to learn about human relationships in that country and the evils of brainwashing and racialism.

The people I called friends and others with whom I came into contact and liked were good, decent people who had no personal experience or knowledge of how the majority lived and suffered. They based their opinions entirely on local radio and newspaper information and on their social contacts with each other. Very few South Africans read international news and they disapproved of the Time magazine because "it is biased." I had the impression that most people did not want their comfort zones disturbed by unpalatable information and consequently they remained in blissful ignorance of the harrowing lives of their black fellow citizens. From personal experience now, I shared the view of Charles Mkhize.

Wisdom began to talk freely to me about his life, his lack of expectations and his political dreams. Those were times when I suspected he was feeling depressed. One morning he was quiet and subdued when setting about his duties so I asked him if everything was o.k. with him.

"Sir, I am sad. I am not sad because I am a black person. I am sad because I can never be more than a servant or an errand boy. White people think blacks are stupid but I know you are different and that is why I can say this to you Sir. I am grateful to have some education and I have to thank Mr. Mkhize for that but even if I had more education, I could not get a better job than this because of job reservation. I like working for you so that is not the trouble. The trouble is that one day I will marry and have children and my children will have the same problems that I have so that makes me sad. I am sad for all black people. I pray every day to Nkulunkulu that before I die, there will be no more apartheid. It is very hard to be happy while you know that you cannot do this and you cannot do that, you cannot go here and you cannot go there. We have to travel on a different bus, always an Indian bus where they do you down. You know how it is, Sir." Yes, I knew how it was.

He had hardly paused for breath and seemed not to expect an answer that would help his cause in anyway. He was in one of his rare viewing-the-world-with-pessimism moods.

Wisdom gave much thought to his future. The fact that he had a job in which he was respected and for which he was well paid, did not blind him to the limitations that he encountered daily and the bleak outlook that black people had to deal with.

I saw in him a lonely, vulnerable boy, a lost soul, far from his home and those dear and familiar to him as he struggled with his fears of what adulthood held for him. I felt immeasurable pity for the youngster who was doing his best to fit in with a foreign lifestyle, to do a good job with no security and no vision for the future. There was nothing for the black kids to do in their off hours, no sporting facilities nearby, nothing to boost their spirits. I shrugged off my sympathy because it would do neither of us any good.

"Yes, Wisdom, I know how it is and I am sorry it is the way it is. Being blue won't help so cheer up. How is Dumisa?" I asked.

Although Wisdom harboured a sense of hopelessness at the political stalemate, he was generally a happier person since we had been to his kraal together. He was less subservient though equally polite and he seemed to appreciate that when he spoke to me on subjects important to him, I listened patiently and understood. I bought 'take-aways' more frequently and one evening as we sat down to enjoy a meal together at the kitchen table he asked me if I had any magazines he could read that would improve his general knowledge.

"Nothing too difficult to begin with" he added with a grin.

I suggested that he start by reading The Witness, the local newspaper that was delivered to my flat every morning. I had developed an uncomfortable sense of responsibility towards Wisdom and his well-being. Uncomfortable, because our time together was limited and what would become of him after that?

"Skivvy I've been thinking", I said one morning as he washed up my breakfast plates,

"You are eighteen now, wouldn't it be a good idea if you got your driver's licence?"

"What? Sir!" He nearly dropped the plate he was drying.

"I'm prepared to pay for you to have driving lessons if you agree to be my chauffeur when I need to be driven somewhere."

Wisdom did not know how to contain his joy, his astonishment nor his excitement.

That was when I started to prepare him for a life when I would no longer be there. He was proud of being a Right Hand Man but it was not a job description that would enable him to find work while with a driver's licence, he could seek employment with a company; the best any black man could hope to achieve in the job market I thought ruefully.

Wisdom had grown taller and had filled out. I noticed that his flat-boy's uniform fitted him better and he looked more mature.

I started inviting out the young women I had met and continued to meet at dinner parties, at Cathedral Peak or at the Country Club and I hoped that one of them might help me to forget Alysha and to realise that in time I could love again. That did not happen but I did not fear that it would never happen.

On reflection, the South African girls were prettier than anywhere else I had been and most of them had good figures. Looks were very important to them.   Their discussions were usually of superficial interests but that meant that they were light-hearted company and at the end of a busy day, that was rather pleasant. During the month preceding the July Handicap in Durban, South Africa's equivalent of Ascot, women spent much time discussing fashions and clothes.

Another annual event that was a highlight and kept them guessing was the Miss South Africa contest as a forerunner to the Miss World in London.   "Do you think Miss Natal or Miss Transvaal will win this year?"

"It's difficult to say. I like Miss Natal. Connie knows Miss Transvaal personally and says she is a beauty but she does not stand a good chance because it is not a contest in stupidity. If it were, she would win hands down."

"That doesn't always count because you know what men are, the male judges overlook intelligence if they are dazzled by the looks. It has a lot to do with sex appeal you know."

"Well, to be fair, it is a beauty contest and not an I.Q. test but the judges are supposed to assess them on both."

To use their own expression, they were a hoot!

The young women were also sports savvy and had a knack for not missing anything on or off the field.

"Felicity was at Kingsmead last week for the Currie Cup and do you know who she saw? Robbie Peterson! He works in Cape Town now and he was with a girl who looks *Coloured*! Can you imagine that of *Robbie Peterson*? He should know better. When you live in the Cape, you have to meet the family first before getting involved and finding out that you cannot get married anyway. Oh well, some people learn the hard way. Pity about that; I always fancied Robbie. He's my type."

"Why can they not get married?" I asked having a reasonably good idea but wanting to hear it from her.

"A Coloured is not allowed to marry a white person! Every person's I.D. card stipulates to which racial group that person belongs. If you apply to get married, you have to produce your I.D. card. There is no getting around that. A person can look white but when you meet the family, you can tell immediately if they are Coloureds. That's why I said Robbie should have met the family first." She said slowly and tolerantly.

"I know about the Immorality Act but I didn't think it extended to Coloureds not being permitted to marry a white person."

"They belong to different racial groups, Silly," she said as though speaking to a half-wit. "Coloureds live mainly in the Cape as a result of Jan van Riebeeck and his cronies in sixteen hundred and so much."

Then there were those young women who spoke without thinking or knew no better, the universal kind. During drinks at the Country Club after a hectic game of tennis one Saturday afternoon, Rosemary a girl in her late twenties suddenly threw a question at me,

"Roger is there any truth in the story that most Englishmen are homosexuals?"

"I have never heard that story." I answered taken aback at the irrelevance of the question.

"They say that boys' public schools in England are breeding grounds for homosexuals."

"I am a product of a boys' public school in England and what 'they say' is news to me. Consequently, I have never had reason to enquire into the matter. I suggest that as it is of interest to you, you should contact the boys' boarding schools here in Natal such as Kearsney College, Hilton College and Michaelhouse. They are all run on the same lines as the public schools in England. Based on the statistics at these schools, you could with reasonable certainty presume that the statistics would be much the same for the public schools in England."

A woman giggled nervously, someone coughed. The schools I had mentioned were the best in the country and a number of men present were ex pupils.

Esmé who had just spoken was normally a shy person and at last she had plucked up courage to say something in public and she feared she had chosen the wrong thing to say! I felt sorry for her. Embarrassed and red as a beet she had sunk into the back of her chair and looked as though she would like to disappear altogether. I concluded that her intention had been less to embarrass me than to impress the others with her avant-garde knowledge.

"All homosexuals should be shot wherever they are," Cyril, the club's tennis champion, announced in a loud, resolute voice that broke the uncomfortable silence. His tone implied that he definitely did not expect anyone to contradict him.

"Do you think there should be a new Act of Parliament?" I asked him facetiously.

"Do you mean an Anti-Homosexual Act?" He took my question seriously.

"Yes, something of that sort." That was my only contribution to the argument that I observed with interest as it gathered momentum.

"Good idea. Homosexuality is a sin against humanity. It is unnatural. You only have to read the Bible."

One of the women, no longer a playing member but someone who loved to watch tennis, volunteered her opinion,

"It comes of easy living and the good life. Take the war years. Men had to be men and no nonsense about it. They never heard of such things in those days."

"That doesn't mean that such things didn't exist," Diana Blake said, "Sexuality is born in us and there must sometimes be deviations from what we consider normal. There is nothing new under the sun and that includes homosexuality." Diana was a flamboyant person obviously not reluctant to sail against the wind in a conversational manner.

"Do you mean to tell me, Diana, that you condone such behaviour?" one of the young women asked incredulously.

"I think you have used the word "condone" inaccurately in this context. I do not pass judgement. I cannot concern myself with what I do not see. I would hate to see a public display of affection between homosexuals just as I hate to see a public display between heterosexuals. Certain behaviour belongs behind closed doors."

Diana stood her ground but the tide of opposition was overwhelming. Her opponents were too focussed, too hostile on the subject so she graciously let go. The consensus was that homosexuality should be banished from the face of the earth!

I admired Diana's courage. It could not have been easy to be a lone voice in that unexpectedly antagonistic group. She was happily married with two children otherwise they probably would have assumed that she belonged to that despised group of sexual perverts.

The aggressive opposition to Diana's opinion illustrated in my opinion the narrow-minded views of the average South African. The majority judged moral situations according to their interpretation of the Bible. I doubted whether many, if any, had read the Bible; they accepted at face value one another's pronouncements and opinions in that respect.

"Anyone for more tennis?" Diana asked hopefully and then it was once again tennis as usual.

When I compared the priorities of life in South Africa with the seriousness of most people's existence in England, it was a refreshing change. In England the average person worried about the National Health, about the exorbitant taxes and the inequality of the educational system, the wealthy worried about the crippling inheritance tax and everyone complained of the weather. South Africa's concerns centred around rugby and cricket. It was pleasant indeed although politics always featured even when the topic was sport.

Sitting at the bar at the country club one Saturday afternoon, I listened to the men discussing the previous week's inter-provincial rugby match, Natal vs. Free State. "Danie played like a mompara. The selectors should drop him from the side."

"Forget it; fat chance of that. He's related to Bram Fourie."

One evening during dinner with Jeremy and Sally, I mentioned my meeting with Boetie and Annabel Pienaar.

"*Not Boetie Pienaar*! He is one of South Africa's most famous landscape artists. You've actually met Boetie Pienaar!"

"You sound impressed Jeremy," I couldn't help teasing him, "Wasn't it you who told me that the Afrikaans and the English-speaking don't fraternize or have high regard for one another?"

"That doesn't alter the fact that he's a brilliant artist. I have never met the man of course but he is reputed to be quite a character. I speak from hearsay."

Six

Wisdom passed his driver's test at the fifth attempt. I was beginning to wonder whether he had any technical aptitude at all. To commemorate his success, I sent him out to buy a chauffeur's uniform and cap. Wisdom was big on uniforms. He was ecstatic. Once again, via, via, via, via friends he knew and friends he knew of, he got the news to Ugogo who in turn told Mr. Mkhize. Charles Mkhize was Wisdom's role model, his hero. His grandmother was, thus far, the only woman he loved.

I bought a take-away and offered Wisdom a glass of wine, something I had never done before and possibly would not do again. We had something to celebrate! He was delighted with the bonsela I gave him.

It was spring, though that made little difference in Natal. The climate was sub tropical so it was always lush with tropical plants and flowering shrubs. The University spring break got underway and I decided to make a trip taking the Garden Route to Cape Town. I had been to Cape Town a number of times on my lecturing tours but had never had the opportunity to sightsee. The seasons were more noticeable in the Cape since the Cape enjoyed a Mediterranean climate. Namaqualand daisies were in full bloom and everyone had told me that it was an unforgettable sight, and it was.

Wisdom, proud as a peacock, did the driving and I was a relaxed passenger since all his lessons had paid off and he was an excellent driver. We took it slowly stopping at important sights that were not to be missed such as the Cango Caves in Oudtshoorn and we visited an ostrich farm. I spent the nights in the best possible hotels and Wisdom stayed in the servants' rooms. I had no idea how good or bad they were and I didn't ask. Wisdom was having the time of his life.

After dinner one evening in a small, family-run hotel in Muizenberg, a beach resort near Cape Town, I went to the bar/ lounge and there I met a Rhodesian couple, Frank and Marion Guthrie. They were the only other people there so we started talking. I enjoyed meeting people in that casual manner as I found it to be the best way of getting to know people from a cross-section of South Africans. The social functions in Maritzburg were always pleasant but I found that those who attended them were of similar mind and interests.

When the Guthries heard that I had been in the country for a short while, they were very keen to tell me about their beloved Rhodesia. I listened attentively to their stories of life there and of the splendid sights that I simply *had* to see before going back to England. They mentioned the Chimanimani Mountains, Inyanga, the Zimbabwe Ruins and the Victoria Falls. They spoke of their homeland with such passion that I asked them why they had left it.

"Marion and I both come from tobacco farming families and when my parents retired, we took over their farm. We loved the life, the only way of life we knew. However, we saw the writing on the wall when the British Government imposed sanctions against Rhodesia at the time of Ian Smith's Unilateral Declaration of Independence. We were fortunate to sell our farm shortly before the tobacco industry went down the drain into final collapse. It will probably never recover. The farmers diversified to other crops but that held no appeal for us. Talk about being sold down the river! It was all due to bloody-mindedness and ignorance of the situation by Harold Wilson. Can't blame the Labour government entirely since the trouble started with Harold Macmillan's "wind of change" speeches as he rushed through Africa. The two Harold's have much to answer for but you know all this. On the bright side, we now breed racehorses in Nottingham Road in Natal and can't complain," he said with a smile. I told them I had been to that area on a short visit and thought it one of the loveliest parts of the Natal midlands.

"Yes it is," Marion said reflectively with a catch in her voice "but we still long for Rhodesia and I suppose that's natural. It is so difficult to forsake one's roots and move away permanently leaving behind home, lifelong friends - people like oneself - a way of life, memories of a lifetime and family history. Our nearest city was Salisbury, surely one of the happiest, most perfect cities on God's earth." Marion was becoming emotional so I quickly intercepted and asked a question of Frank,

"Did you consider farming in this country?" I asked.

"No, tobacco farming is different from anything else and that was my passion. I am now wholeheartedly committed to our new challenge and enjoy it even more than I did tobacco farming! When Marion settles down, I feel sure she too will see that this is an excellent alternative to tobacco." He spoke with eagerness and optimism that I admired because leaving everything behind in Rhodesia must have been as stressful for him as it had been for her.

We said goodnight after exchanging addresses and they made me promise that I would visit them when next in their area. I said I would rather they invited me when it suited them. They convinced me that the Vic Falls was "a must see."

South Africans called Rhodesians "Whenwes" because the ex Rhodesians usually got sentimental about their country and talked a lot about "when we ....." I suppose Marion and Frank were typical examples and who could blame them.

Wisdom and I spent a few days in Cape Town and went to the top of Table Mountain in the cable car. "I was knocked for six," as Boetie would have said, that the attendant allowed Wisdom to accompany us in the cable car because I had become accustomed to the ins and outs of apartheid and had expected that he would have to wait for me at the bottom. Wisdom said the reason for this was that he was wearing his chauffeur's uniform. I was beginning to recognise the importance of what Wisdom tried subtly and persistently to drum into me; a uniform was of the utmost importance in all situations.

The experience was memorable especially the fabulous views of the city and beyond that the Indian and Atlantic Oceans. The guide told us that we were very fortunate to have such a clear view because sometimes the clouds moved in and very little could be seen of the city and sea below.

We arrived back in Maritzburg in time for the start of the new term.

There was a pile of post awaiting my attention and, amongst it, an envelope addressed to me in very familiar handwriting. It was from Alysha. My initial reaction surprised me. It was one of ambivalence. I had accepted the situation. What could we possibly hope to achieve by having further contact except to re-open painful wounds. On the other hand, my heartbeat did not only quicken, it raced like crazy.

"Skivvy", I called through to the kitchen, "please make me a pot of tea and bring my slippers." I settled down in comfort to read the contents of the letter.

My darling Roger,

Your visit was a wonderful surprise but when you left, I felt that everything important in my life had gone with you. I could not settle to anything and only my job at the University kept me on an even keel so purposely I worked long and intensive hours.

Ma and Pitajee talked for a long time after you left but I didn't join them. Finally, Ma came into my suite and told me that they liked you very much and that they were distressed on my behalf. She said she fully understood because if she were younger, she might have fallen for you herself. She loved your cultured English voice. That was all very complimentary and I'm sure Ma meant what she said, but I know her well and to win someone over, she goes to great lengths to understand their point of view perfectly and then comes up with the inevitable BUT…!

Ma told me that you phoned me a number of times after your arrival in South Africa and they decided it best not to pass your messages on to me. I wept when I heard of their shameless deceit. What must you have thought of me?

I now have a suggestion to make and Ma and Pitajee are finally in agreement with it, albeit *very* reluctantly. I suppose at a certain stage all parents have to let go of their children, let them make their own mistakes and watch with bated breath what they imagine to be total lunacy. They think I'm out of my mind while I have always been *so* sensible, they tell me sadly and I know they feel wretched about it. But I have to follow my heart and my heart is with you.

When the long summer vacation starts, how about you and I going to England together (on separate flights of course) so that I can see if I could settle down and live in the U.K.? A trip like that should provide the answer to what we so desperately yearn to know; can we, under all the negative circumstances, plan a future together or is it best that we don't even try?

If, in the meantime, you have decided that the complications as outlined by Pitajee are insurmountable obstacles to our being happy together, please do not hesitate to let me know because then I will be able to move on with my life.

From your loving,
Alysha.

I was certainly surprised at the contents of Alysha's letter and had to read it twice to let it sink in. Gone was my ambivalence! She suggested that we might still have a future together! In England, no woman of her age and academic standing would need the approval of her parents before taking such a decision but this was not England and the circumstances were vastly different.

Planning a fortnight's holiday in England with Alysha was the best thing that had happened in a long time. It was unfortunate that we would be there in the winter because it would be her first visit to Britain and I wanted her love it.

We had not seen each other for a few months, not since I had visited her home, but after our exchange of letters, we phoned regularly. We dared not risk a meeting in case something went wrong and our relationship might be exposed.

I travelled to England the night before Alysha and booked in at Grosvenor House where we would be staying. Our accommodation was perfect, two bedrooms en suite with a sitting room between them. I ordered flowers for her bedroom and there was a bowl of fruit in our sitting room, courtesy of the hotel.

In great excitement, I was up very early the next morning to meet Alysha at Heathrow and when she came through Customs, I gasped at the sight of her. She was wearing a cream mink coat with hood that framed her face and her dark hair. She was a captivating sight. Many heads turned and finally she whispered,

"Even here people look at us; a white man with an Indian woman." I assured her that their stares had nothing to do with her colour or mine but with her extraordinary beauty. That was certainly true. She looked like a glamorous film star but without the egocentricity and the publicity-seeking agenda of famous screen idols.

We drove straight to the hotel and Alysha never having seen snow before was enthralled with the scene around us. It had been midsummer in sub tropical Durban so the contrast in climate was extreme. When we arrived at the hotel, the concierge welcomed Alysha with his customary friendliness and asked whether she would like tea or coffee sent to the suite.

"Tea please."

"And an English breakfast for two." I added. I, for one, was starving.

The porter delivered her luggage and then with all that had taken place, we were strangely ill at ease never having been in that situation before but our discomfort did not last for long - we were together at last!

On the third day of our holiday, we were on our way to the village of Knaresborough in Yorkshire when we saw a quaint, thatched pub, "The Spotted Dog" and decided to have an English pub lunch. We went inside and saw that a log fire was burning in the fireplace. The pub was at least a hundred and fifty years old with a typically old English interior. It would have been dark inside had it not been for the subdued lighting. The atmosphere on that cold day was warm, friendly and welcoming.

We had just given our order when Alysha, unexpectedly serious, said that she had something important to discuss with me. She had been light-hearted all morning so what was coming? I waited.

"I was awake for some hours last night thinking of our relationship." She began earnestly and as she hesitated, I began to feel anxious.

"We love each other and neither of us desires any other partner in life. If we could marry we would, but that is out of the question while your contract binds you to South Africa." She paused and I feared that she was going to end our romance at least temporarily and my heart sank. Silently, I waited for her to continue.

"We are enjoying this wonderful opportunity to be together privately and in public without fear of the law and since this is an exceptional situation for us to be in, I think our time together should also be without frustration. I am twenty-seven so it is not as though I am too young to take a sensible decision in this respect. I am happy for us to consummate our love."

I breathed again. Relief! Hardly able to believe what she had just said, except that she had been so serious that there could be no doubting it, I took her hands in mine, leaned over and kissed her without a thought as to who might be watching us. I hardly knew what to say. From the point of view of how little time we had actually spent together, I could hardly have expected this though I had hoped for it. The thought of making love to Alysha …! I called to the barman to serve us his best champagne and a glass for every customer in the pub.

The barman, probably also the owner, round and jolly, laughed and said, "And a bottle on the house!"

The guests in the pub, about twenty in all, assumed that I had proposed to Alysha and that she had accepted. They congratulated us and everyone began introducing themselves to us and to each other. When all the glasses were charged they sang, "For they are jolly good fellows …." A party was underway. Was this the traditional reserve of the British I wondered!

At about three o'clock, still in a state of euphoria, I asked the barman confidentially if there was a good jeweller in the area and he wrote down the name and address of one he could highly recommend. I followed his directions and when I parked the car in front of a small row of shops, Alysha was completely taken by surprise. I guided her into the shop and while an assistant tactfully distracted her, the owner asked me what price range I had in mind and then produced a tray of sparkling rings. Alysha, at first overwhelmed by the suddenness of all that was happening, recovered her emotional equilibrium and chose an eye-catching, glittering ring, a band of rubies and diamonds.

In the otherwise unromantic setting of our hired car, I put the ring on her finger and that sealed the permanence of our relationship. We were ecstatic.

We drove back to Grosvenor House agreeing that it was the happiest day of our lives. When the lift stopped at our floor, I picked Alysha up to carry her if not over the threshold, then at least into our suite.

"Whose bedroom? Yours or mine?" I asked still holding her firmly in my arms.

"You're the boss!" she laughed happily.

"Then to the nearest one!"

Our days – and nights -were joyous.

I showed Alysha many of the tourist attractions in and around London and since the summer tourists had gone, we were able to admire everything at our leisure. We went to a number of West End shows and dined in trendy restaurants in Soho. We went to museums and cathedrals and we made trips to Oxford and other towns of interest. Alysha had never travelled on the Underground so everything was exciting and new for her.

I had told my parents that we would stay with them in Devon for the last weekend before returning to South Africa thinking that if there was any awkwardness, we could leave without there being hurt feelings and if not, we could choose to stay for two more days. Alysha was nervous about meeting my parents though I assured her that she need not be and when I introduced her to them, they were friendly and welcomed her warmly. They gave a dinner party on Saturday night to which they had invited my brothers and their wives so it was a real family evening with animated conversation and much to my relief, they were all interested to meet Alysha and make her feel at home.

I had always been close to my mother, as close as mother and son can be considering that since I became a teenager, our lives together were dependent on school holidays. I was sensitive to her moods so I knew that while she did and said all the right things, she was not her usual composed self and she avoided eye contact with me. I wondered whether she was perhaps suffering pangs of jealousy that one hears is common when a mother senses that she's about to lose her youngest son to another woman. Was she thinking that I could have, and should have done better! Could it be that Alysha, dressed in her saris instead of western dress, was just a little too exotic for my mother to feel comfortable with or, heaven forbid, was my mother a racialist after all? We can never know such things about others not even those closest to us. I remembered Mr. Patel's observations about the British. To give credit where it was due, if Mum was struggling with conflicting emotions for whatever reason then she was doing exceptionally well in hiding the fact from others. I was grateful to her for that.

We left on Monday morning as originally planned and that was not for any reason of awkwardness but simply that our holiday was almost at an end and we wanted to be together and alone for the remaining time.

As we drove away, Alysha asked,

"Do you think your family liked me? They were all very friendly but it must have been quite daunting for them, particularly for your parents, to meet a prospective Indian in-law."

"There is no doubt that they liked you and don't forget I had told them about you and that you were a South African Indian so that was no surprise to them," I answered in all honesty. "I think that if I had discussed our relationship with them, their reaction would have been similar to your parents regarding culture and lifestyle. But I did not discuss us with them and they would not have expected me to do so."

I could not imagine anyone not liking Alysha.

We had two days left of our holiday in England. It was so cold that we were happy to spend most of our time in the hotel. Every minute together was becoming ever more precious as our departure drew nearer. If our holiday had proved anything at all, it was not only that we wanted to spend the rest of our lives together but we knew that we belonged together.

Alysha had enjoyed our holiday immensely but she could not imagine settling down happily to life in England. Being on holiday in a country, she said, was so different from living there. Two weeks had been long enough in that climate! Nothing was familiar to her and she knew she would be terribly homesick. I could understand her feelings because Britain was so unlike South Africa and India the only two countries she had experienced before this visit. We had to count England out in our search for a country that we could call home.

I suggested to Alysha that our next holiday should be to India. Perhaps we would find our niche there depending on what job opportunities were available to us. Neither of us had a clue about that but it gave us something to think about and work towards.

We knew we would not be able to live happily from one holiday to the next without seeing each other in between so we would have to be ingenious and get around the laws that attempted to criminalise us.

I saw Alysha off at Heathrow the night before I was due to leave and the tears trickled down her cheeks through a brave smile as she turned to give a final wave with one hand, her hand-luggage in the other.

Seven

Wisdom had gone to his kraal on holiday while I was away and I had instructed him to be back in time to open the flat, clean it and air it on the day before my return. I fully expected him to be in Maritzburg when I got there. Instead of that, I caught sight of him when I went through the Exit at Louis Botha airport in Durban. He was wearing his chauffeur's uniform and cap and was standing with a few other 'non-whites.' The sight of Wisdom and his happy familiar face, the bright sunshine and the eternally blue sky, gave me the strangest feeling that I had arrived home.

A different pattern of life followed our return from England and only those who have the stomach for danger, for intrigue and the consequent excitement and fear generated from it, could have coped coolly with the situation in which we found ourselves. Neither Alysha nor I had those qualities so we were uncomfortable living our cat and mouse existence. We had no choice though; we felt that we were married already and a separation at that stage would have been unthinkable. I began to feel that we were exaggerating the circumstances; surely the police had more important matters on hand than to spy on our every movement. Of what importance could we possibly be in the greater scheme of things? When I mentioned that to Alysha, she assured me that any suspicion of the contravention of apartheid rules were very important in the greater scheme of things! In the full knowledge of all that was at stake, we took our chances. How immeasurable were the risks that we were prepared to take to see each other.

When I arrived home one evening, Wisdom told me that Dr. Govender had phoned and left a message for me to return his call after seven o'clock that night if possible. The name was familiar and then I remembered Alysha mentioning that Goofy Govender, an oncologist, and his wife Mira who were amongst her best friends.

I phoned and after initial introductions and small talk, he told me that Alysha had told them of our romantic involvement and that above all else we wanted to get married as soon as we could. In order for us to be able to see each other, he suggested that we meet at his house under certain conditions.

He proposed that I travel to his home at about six-thirty on Sunday mornings when there would be no one about. On arrival, I should drive straight into his garage. I could then spend the day with them and Alysha would either be there or get there later. That was a minor detail as long as there was no pattern to her comings and goings. He gave me his address and directions of how to get to his house.

"This is extremely generous of you. Won't you be running a risk yourself?"

"I must admit it was Mira's idea. No, the risk is all yours. It is not as though we are harbouring a criminal although you would certainly think so by the way the regime rules this country. We shall talk at length about this when you are here. I'm sure you have discovered by now that every South African whatever his colour or identification, is obsessed with the topic of politics and nothing ever improves in this respect, it only gets worse."

"Thanks a million. I am looking forward to meeting you. Will it be o.k. if I come this Sunday?"

"Sure thing. I'll see you then and in the meantime, Mira will arrange other details with Alysha." I felt exhilarated at the prospect of seeing Alysha in normal circumstances.

I arrived on the dot of six. Mira and Goofy's house was modern, designed so that the expansive views were visible from ceiling to floor sliding glass doors that stretched across the entire width of the front of the house. The furnishings too were contemporary without a trace of Indian culture. The paintings were attractive for those who appreciated modern art, bright splashes of colour. Mira and Goofy's home reflected not only their taste in interior decoration, but also their independent thinking in a modern world. Theirs had not been an arranged marriage. They met and fell in love at the hospital where they both worked and although they had a traditional Hindu wedding their parents had played no part in their choice of partner. Fortunately, they said, when the families met, everyone was happy.

"We told them they should be grateful to us for saving them the hassle of advertising, searching for suitable consorts, quite apart from the expense of it all!" laughed Mira.

By experiencing romantic love themselves, they had gained understanding of our love that transcended all human obstacles and restrictions.

Alysha and I enjoyed their company and the company of their friends who often visited them. No one showed any obvious curiosity when they were introduced to me. Mira took great pride in her secluded garden that was screened off from the road by poinsettia. Goofy and Mira insisted that our rendezvous at their home did not inconvenience them but we did not want to become a burden so every now and again, we skipped a Sunday. Those were blissful, carefree times when were able to be together without anxiety, without fear of being discovered, Everything went well for weeks on end until one Thursday evening Wisdom told me that Mdala wanted to speak to me in confidence. "No one must know," he added.

I had met Mdala only once. It was difficult to judge his age. He might well have been in his mid fifties and to Wisdom, of course, that was ancient. Mdala's hair was turning grey and his face was deeply lined but there was youthfulness about him and his eyes were alert. Unlike the other flat boys, he wore long trousers instead of shorts but otherwise his uniform was identical to theirs with the red trimming. I told Wisdom to invite Mdala to come to my flat at any time that suited him, as I would not be going out that evening.

Mdala came to my door with a gloomy expression. I invited him into the kitchen and offered him a cup of tea that he declined with much embarrassment but he agreed to sit down and we faced each other across the kitchen table.

"Baas, I've come to tell you of danger. Every Sunday morning when you leave the flats at six o'clock, people stand under the trees and watch you and they write things down. I don't like it. Maybe they are the police. I do not know who they are. I want to tell you to be careful because they might make trouble for you."

"Mdala, I don't like the sound of what you tell me. I cannot imagine that my movements are interesting to anyone. Are they black people or white people?"

"Baas, everyone standing under the trees and writing down, is a mlungu, everyone." Mlungu I knew was a white man. I had picked up a few Zulu words.

"I have nothing to hide, Mdala, so I am not worried about them but it is strange behaviour. Thank you for telling me. I will watch out for them if you think they are up to no good."

"They are, Sir."

I took his warning seriously and was worried by what he had told me. The idea that the police might be on to us and were watching my every movement was a sobering thought.

I phoned Alysha from the university the next morning to say that we should change our Sunday routine. She too was anxious about Mdala's message and together we decided that I should not visit her for the next month.

I could not settle to anything for long. I felt as I did when I was a child and was struggling with a guilty conscience over some minor transgression except that now this was no minor matter. Sunday loomed ahead and I dreaded being alone with my thoughts as much as I dreaded the idea of being alone on a crowded beach. I phoned Boetie and said that I would be at a loose end on Sunday and if it suited them, I would like to visit that day.

"We'll expect you for lunch, Old Boy. Just a minute, the girls are calling something. They say to bring your cozzie."

Boetie calling me Old Boy was amusing. I smiled despite my cheerlessness. I had to ask what a cozzie was and learned that I had to take my swimming trunks. So the girls had heard about me.

My spirits lifted as soon as I drove off to spend the day with Boetie and Annabel. Nottingham Road was a pleasant, rural area in the Natal Midlands and I was pleased to be going back there to enjoy the company of my new friends. I met the three girls, Darlene, Charlene and Pauline. They were gangly teenagers, but I could see the potential and that they would turn out to be attractive one day. They all had fair hair, so unlike both parents. We talked briefly. They said they would see me later and then went back to join their friends in the pool.

"Boetie," I said, "I have heard from a friend of mine that you are one of South Africa's most famous landscape painters. I wonder if you would mind showing me some of your paintings. I would like to buy one before going back to England."

"Come off it, Roger. You will not be going back to England. This is God's own country. With all our ruddy problems, there is no place like this anywhere. This is paradise. Follow me and I'll show you my studio and a few unfinished works. Up to now, as soon as I finish a few paintings, I sell them to galleries. I have these dollies of mine to keep in style."

I followed Boetie down a winding path, passed the swimming pool to the end of his wooded five-acre property where his studio was located beside a natural pool. Reeds grew in and around the water and there were birds in abundance. Indeed, it was a paradise.

I followed him into his studio, a light and airy room. I could see his work, unfinished though it was, was exceptional and I hoped to be able to buy a painting of the Drakensberg when he had one available. I hoped it might be of Cathedral Peak. I mentioned it just to be sure that I would be first in line! Without getting to know Boetie better, one would never suppose with his macho exterior that he was a man of great artistic talent; a person sensitive to beauty in nature and people.

All of a sudden I had an exciting idea.

"Do you paint portraits or do you stick to landscapes?" I asked.

"I've painted Annabel and the girls a few times but I lose myself in landscapes."

"I'm going to ask you a favour and please be frank if you would rather not do it. I would like to have a painting of Wisdom, my man servant. May I commission you to paint him? You see, Wisdom typifies for me a special aspect of life in this country. Although you predict that I will not leave South Africa, I'm afraid I have little choice because my professional ambitions cannot be realised here."

My request had little to do with Wisdom representing a special aspect of life in South Africa. I would have enough reminders of that. It had everything to do with Wisdom himself and I did not know whether Boetie would understand that.

Wisdom's and my relationship was multifaceted due to circumstances. He was my servant but he was also a young friend and I regarded him with paternal concern. His life was tough and would get tougher in the future because he was black in a racialist society and I sympathised with that. He was a good person, honest, sincere and naïve in a disarming way and I worried about what would become of him when I left. I guess I loved him in the same way as a man might love his foster son.

"I will be pleased to do it for you. Send me a couple of photos of him taken at different angles. Better still, bring them yourself."

Wisdom posed happily for the photographs and as soon as our local photographer had developed them, I posted them to Boetie.

About a week after my visit to Boetie and Annabel, my phone was dead. I could not understand it because I always paid my accounts on time. I reported the fault to the Telephone Exchange and contrary to their tardy reputation; mechanics came the next day to repair the lines. Wisdom said they had worked on the bedroom phone and on the sitting room phone. I happened to mention that when I made my daily phone call to Alysha from the university.

Mr. Patel phoned me almost immediately and asked me to meet him urgently at his business address in Grey Street, Durban, and suggested Saturday at 2 o'clock. I was not to mention the meeting to anyone and there were to be no more phone calls to his home or to Alysha at the university.

Something serious must have cropped up.

As agreed, I arrived at Mr. Patel's business address at two o'clock. Once inside the building I discovered that he was the Owner and Managing Director of a large import/export company with dealings mainly in India. On meeting him for the first time, one could see that he was an influential person but on the only other occasion that I had met him, we had a more personal topic to discuss than business.

I announced myself and the receptionist phoned through to say that I had arrived. An efficient-looking Asian woman greeted me, said that she was Mr. Patel's secretary and asked me to follow her. She took me to a small, private sitting room and said that Mr. Patel would join me shortly. Only minutes later, Alysha's father came into the room, greeted me rather tersely and seated himself opposite me.

"Good afternoon, Roger, I'll get straight to the point. I am having sleepless nights and want to put you fully in the picture as I see it. This situation between you and Alysha cannot continue. I understand that you love each other but sometimes love demands too high a price and this is one of those times.

First of all, about the boss-boy at your block of flats: he may be genuine and he may not be. The police have their informers in every corner of society and they pay them well. He may well be an informer. In this capacity, he would have observed your comings and goings and have reported them to the police. It could be that he is now responsible for finding out where you go to at that time in the morning. By gaining your confidence, he can learn the most. I am pleased you gave nothing away. Please never do. No one can be trusted in this country. Perhaps I am doing him a grave injustice but we cannot know that and we cannot take chances.

Secondly, your phone being out of order and then repaired in record time is in itself most suspicious. That never happens. My guess is that the mechanics have installed a recorder so that it will be possible to tap your phone, all incoming and outgoing calls.

I would suggest that you go out tomorrow morning at six o'clock and go to the beachfront for breakfast. Do the same the following week but go somewhere else. Take them all on a wild goose-chase but do not give up going out at that time on Sunday mornings, not for the time being anyway. If you suddenly stop making your early morning trips because of the flat-boy's warning, it will be tantamount to an admission of guilt."

"Mr. Patel, coming from a country where freedom of movement and freedom of speech are civil rights, I find this beyond belief. I hope with all due respects that you are not becoming paranoid about Alysha and me. I can well understand your concern but this sounds highly implausible."

"Believe me, it is not!" he said in exasperation.

"I enjoy going out early in the morning so I will continue to do so. I may even buy a motorbike to make the most of the fresh and invigorating early hours." I was surprised that I said that because I had never considered the possibility of riding a motorbike.

"I know how you feel Mr. Patel; you would like the problem to disappear and me along with it. Occasionally, I do too. The trouble is that Alysha and I love each other, a love that we will never be able to forget. If we give in to external pressures and go our separate ways, we will live with regrets forever. This is the only country in the world, as far as I know, that legislates such personal choices so once my contract ends, we will leave South Africa and get married come what may. When the time comes, I hope we will have your blessing. We have discussed going on holiday to India together to have time alone and to explore the possibility of our marrying and living there if we see career opportunities in that country. How do you feel about that? I will leave this to you and Alysha to decide upon, since as two South Africans, you know so much better than I do what the dangers of that can be. In my ignorance, I see none regarding a holiday together and do not wish of course to see any. I must admit that in general I have begun to feel distrustful of an ominous unknown. I have never before experienced the sensation of fearing an unseen, intangible enemy.

We shook hands, I not knowing what their decision would be and feeling that the emotional seesaw was getting us all down.

That night I looked around my flat and felt ill at ease. I was not fearful of anyone breaking in or causing me physical harm but the idea that I was being stalked by an unseen enemy was unnerving. I could deal with tapped phones by being careful of what I said and to whom I spoke. However, the idea that hidden cameras were probably beamed on me to record my every action was abhorrent and not far removed from the tactics employed by the Russian Communists whom the government and citizens professed to hate and fear with a vengeance.

In deference to Mr. Patel's wishes and his anxiety of the unpleasant consequences should our relationship be exposed, I decided not make the first move to contact Alysha. I knew that her father would have spoken to her in the same stern way that he had spoken to me and that we would have to be cautious and patient.

My days were busy and full. I could not complain either of my social life at the club and with the people I knew. However, when it was dark and quiet at night, my fantasies were of Alysha, of her soft and beautiful body next to mine. I longed to make love to her and to know that she would be there in the morning and every morning for the rest of our lives. I let my imagination run riot as I visualized our living a life together and being together always. When I was in an optimistic mood, I felt sure that that would happen one day. We simply had to survive without cracking up and without the arm of the law pouncing suddenly and unexpectedly. In the meantime, my nonchalant allusion to owning a motorbike became an obsessive idea.

Eight

On the first Saturday following my visit to Mr. Patel's office, I went to a dealer to learn as much as I could about motorbikes. I had not expected them to be so expensive. I asked about taking lessons and followed a crash course. Once I had my licence, I shopped around and finally decided to buy a yellow, black and silver Harley Davidson. The sales clerk told me that it was an exceptional colour combination and they, in the business, had never seen a Harley Davidson like it. They were usually black and silver. I paid for the most expensive and prestigious motorbike on the market.

Wisdom was so impressed that I asked him if he would like a ride on the back of the bike. Then I wondered if I was breaking the law! I was becoming as obsessed as everyone else was with Apartheid.

"Skivvy" I said," I'm going to buy you a helmet and when I take you out you must wear your white shirt and black trousers so that no one can see you are black!"

"Sir, I don't think that is important on a bike. I would never go on the back of a bike in my flat-boys uniform and not in my chauffeur's uniform either." I did not comment further on the topic of uniforms knowing Wisdom's partiality to them. He would be sure to find the correct uniform for riding on the back of a motor bike.

On the next Sunday morning, Wisdom was at my front door, dressed and ready for an early morning ride. We went to Midmar Dam, a large dam on the Umgeni River not far from Maritzburg that was used mainly for water sports. We ate the sandwiches I had prepared the night before and we had a flask of tea with us. Then we rode round the dam that was coupled with a game park. We saw different types of buck grazing and in the distance wildebeest. Nothing was open at that early hour which pleased me since I still felt embarrassed that I could not take Wisdom to any public place. I knew that when we returned, he would delight in telling his buddies, the flat boys, about his latest experience. I had noticed that Wisdom was not above a bit of bragging and from what I had heard of Mdala I wondered how that went down with him.

Then I did something that was unlike anything I had ever done before, that I had to laugh at myself. I joined the Harley Davidson Motorbike Club of Pietermaritzburg. The club organised Sunday morning breakfast runs and I signed up immediately. We met at 6 o'clock in the morning.

To set off with a group of some twenty riders on a wide-open road with no other traffic in sight, to feel the early morning air, the warmth and sight of the rising sun when shades from orange to pink suffused the horizon, was unforgettable. I went to places I would never otherwise have seen and met people I would never otherwise have met. I looked forward eagerly to those mornings and to the companionship of people from different walks of South African life, white walks that is.

We were a dissimilar group of people. Must tell Jeremy I thought; we were whites from different language groups and with different accents, there were Afrikaners, English, two Italians and a Greek. All were South African born except for me. We got on like a house on fire. Occupations too were vastly different. I had submitted mine as "teacher". Daniel was a doctor, Koen owned a smallholding and Dieter was an accountant, Philip a plumber, Luigi onyx marble expert and self-styled business executive, Horatio, a pop star. (We never found out whether Horatio was his real name) and Melvin (Mel) was a garage mechanic. We had one thing in common, our pride in ownership and love of a Harley Davidson. I was not at the point yet of loving my machine but I was certainly proud of it and I was fast becoming hooked on the sport.

The person I most admired in the club was concert pianist, Demetrios, the Greek. His life-story was inspirational. One Sunday morning when we stopped for breakfast at the Valley of A Thousand Hills, one of the most beautiful scenic views in Natal, I asked Demetrios if he would mind telling us how he had become a famous pianist. Everyone was interested to hear his story so we sat around in the long dry grass and listened attentively.

"My parents arrived from Athens shortly before I was born and they opened a small grocery shop in a poor suburb of Johannesburg," he told us. "They were hard working, very devoted parents who despite their battle to make ends meet provided me with a stable, happy childhood. When I was fourteen, I had to leave school for financial reasons and find employment. With not much more than a primary school education, my chances of getting a job, one that I liked or wanted, were zero. I had to take whatever I could get.

A friend of my fathers owned a boxing stable and he offered to take me under his wing and train me. Because I was tall for my age and sturdily built, he said there might be prospects for me in that line of business.

Boxing was so far from the dream I had of becoming a pianist that I cried myself to sleep for nights on end.

What could be more senseless than fighting simply to inflict pain, injury and preferably, a knock out on someone with whom I had no axe to grind? In addition, I certainly did not relish the idea of someone battering me around. I was not brave enough to endure that sort of physical suffering for no good reason. I could not think of anything worse than being a boxer.

I started training with three other boys of the same age. I thought I would go crazy with the brainless hours of punching a bag, skipping, running and weight lifting only to end the day with sparring matches. In desperation, seeking understanding and above all advice, I went to see our Priest."

"Could he help you? What advice did he give you?" I asked intensely interested in what a Priest would advise in the circumstances. What advice could anyone give?

"He encouraged me to become the most accomplished boxer I possibly could and said that whatever I undertook in life I should do to the best of my ability. He suggested that I save every cent possible from what I earned and he told me who to approach for piano lessons. Looking back, he must have been instrumental in that because lessons from a top-class teacher could not have come at the price I paid per lesson. My teacher told me where I could go to practise and I paid an hourly rate for playing the piano. The lessons and the time I spent practising were the joy of my existence. Every now and again, my teacher gave me a free lesson and that enabled me to pay for more practise hours.

I boxed my heart out. I never joined in with the social life of the boxers, because not only did I hardly have time to do so, but also I had very little in common with them except that we all did the same things like punching a bag day after day. They were decent fellows who, like me, had not had other career opportunities available to them. Their conversations were always of politics and sex and they knew nothing of either." He smiled, remembering with amusement his innocent young colleagues.

He went on to tell us that when his music teacher considered the time right, he entered Demetrios in a countrywide piano recital competition. Demetrios won the competition, a money prize and a bursary for further study. He lived on a shoestring but he was able to give up boxing and his career took off. He and his teacher were like father and son and both benefited from a personal as well as professional relationship in which they could share their love and knowledge of music. His teacher still lived in Johannesburg and Demetrios spent time with him whenever he was in the city and that was often.

I was deeply moved whenever I attended one of Demetrios's concerts. He was on a different plane when he played the piano lost in a world of music. Sometimes he caressed the keys with tender affection, his touch so soft and gentle that the music stirred one's soul even of those who like me had no special affinity with music or musical instruments. When the music demanded it, he played with fire and passion. Then his fingers moved with lightning speed and dexterity hitting dozens of keys up and down the keyboard in a manner that seemed physically impossible. My admiration was as much for the character of the man on the podium as it was for the joy he bestowed on all who listened to him playing.

One Sunday morning in midsummer when it was particularly hot and humid despite the earliness of the hour, we of the Harley Davidson club stopped for breakfast where we could shelter in the shade of a few big trees. Big trees were not easy to find off the beaten track where there was mainly dense undergrowth or nothing at all but long grass. Finally we succeeded. Breakfast was our social time and that morning Koen announced that he would be thirty-five years old the next Saturday.

"Ag, it's no big deal but the wife wants me to invite you all to come to a braaivleis to celebrate. The family will be there. Let me know if any of you can make it."

Twelve of us could make it and we agreed to meet at five o'clock at the Show Grounds. Dieter knew the way to Koen's place and would lead us there.

It was a hot evening when we set off from our meeting point. We left the main road and travelled along dirt roads to Koen's home about ten miles from Pietermaritzburg. As we approached his small holding, we experienced the peacefulness of a rural scene. There were a few cattle grazing in a field, there was a fowl-run near the house and there was a healthy looking vegetable garden with an overhead sprinkler system that gave a cooling effect as it sprayed the plants.

The noise of our twelve motorbikes must have heralded our arrival from a distance and generated much interest because excited barefoot children had gathered on the lawn to watch our arrival. I was accustomed to the habit of South African children never wearing shoes except to school or 'going out' and if they wore anything at all on their feet during their leisure time it was 'slip slops.' They seemed awestruck by the sight of so many motorbikes arriving en masse and they greeted us politely in Afrikaans. I deducted then that it was to be an Afrikaans-speaking evening and wondered how it would work out for me as I was a descendant of their historical enemy dating back to the Boer War.

We congratulated Koen on his birthday and he led us followed by the inquisitive children, to the back of the house where there were at least forty other guests. He announced our names individually to the group and suggested that we introduce ourselves to people as we met them. I followed Dieter's example and said, "Roger Sinclair, aangename kennis" as I shook hands with each person I met.

"Koen, you said only family members would be here," I remarked surprised at the numbers.

"Ja, that's right. Man, are we pleased Ouma felt up to it. She is eighty-eight. Tantes, ooms, cousins, nephews and nieces; they're all here."

A suckling pig was turning slowly on a spit and a barbecue fire glowed in a drum cut in half lengthways and suspended between two solid supports. There was a long trestle table bedecked with piles of crockery, cutlery and paper napkins. When darkness fell at about six-thirty someone turned on 'fairy lights,' different coloured lamps that had been strung from the house encircling the braai area. A few helpers placed candles in large brown paper bags on the ground for added lighting and effect I guessed. It was a typically warm African night with an atmosphere to match as we sat under the stars eating the delicious meat and the traditional dishes that accompanied it.

Someone called to André to get his concertina,

"Kom André, kom op met jou concertina!" and then the singing began. I liked the rhythm of the catchy Afrikaans music and planned to buy recordings of the songs that were sung that night such as Saris Marais and Suikerbossie. I caught on quickly to Zulu Warrior with its constantly repeated 'I zicka zimba, zimba, zimba...' Another favourite was Die Alabama.

Tante Koba was asked to sing a solo, "Ag pleez Daddy take us to the drive in..." Singing an English song in her very strong South African accent as was the intention of the songwriter, Jeremy Taylor, was a truly hilarious listening experience because it was a satire on everyday South African life and everyone could identify with the words and the message. An encore was called for and we laughed as much the second time round as we did the first.

I had seldom heard anyone play the piano accordion before that evening. André was a born entertainer who played with untiring energy and an engaging, infectious smile. Clearly no one enjoyed it more than he did. I wouldn't have missed that fun evening for anything and was grateful to be part of an Afrikaans social occasion where extended family members of all ages were automatically part of "the family."

Breakfast runs with my club friends were weekly events that I looked forward to with keen anticipation. They were times when I felt free and happy. However, when we saw something particularly beautiful in nature, either a magnificent view or a flock of birds at sunrise then in those awestruck moments, I was overcome by unexpected, piercing loneliness that had nothing to do with being alone. I was in the company of interesting, uncomplicated people but the feeling was difficult to shake off. I knew the reason for my moments of melancholy – I missed Alysha. I longed for her to be part of my life.

I knew I was living on a time-bomb that would be set off as soon as I made a false move. That false move would be to see Alysha. How spineless I felt when I faced the truth; the government with its laws and threats scared the shit out of people and I was one of them. I had become a wretched victim of the psychosis of those who designed and enforced the crazy laws of the land.

One morning when I was unable to start my car because of a flat battery, I rode my bike to Varsity and in no time at all a group of students had gathered around.

"Hey, Prof, half the girls swoon over you already, what are you doing to us now?" The so-called swooning girls were not one bit interested in my motorbike but the fellows were genuinely impressed. I seemed to have acquired a macho image amongst them. From then on, riding my motorbike to work became a habit to which no one paid any attention after the first few days. I used my car less and less.

Now and again in the evenings, I took Wisdom for a ride. I asked him once what he did in his spare time. He said he went into the township with his friend Dumisa. From what I gathered, the youngsters spent their leisure hours and their money in shebeens. I guessed the shebeen was a social meeting place for them. I knew he sent money to Ugogo every month and spent very little on himself.

One morning Wisdom asked me if I would please take Mdala for a ride on the back of my motorbike. I said I would if Mdala could make it on Tuesday afternoon at about four o'clock. Duly at that time, Mdala arrived at my front door wearing his smartest clothes and Wisdom's helmet. He was a humorous sight but I kept a straight face. He was delighted to sit behind me but clung on for dear life and I realised that he was scared to death. He had never been on, or in, any vehicle other than a bus. On our safe return at the end of an hour's ride, he thanked me with a wide and relieved smile. Seeing how grateful he was, I asked how many flat-boys there were and he said six.

"Do you think they would like to take turns and all have a ride on my motorbike? He hesitated and then said,

"Sir, I will have to think about it."

"I'll leave it to you and if you think it's a good idea, please let me know because I'm sure to forget.

"Thank you Sir." He must have heard from Wisdom that he should call me Sir instead of Baas. Mdala's reluctance to include the others was probably due to the fact that he would then be unable to bask in the image he wished to project, that of Boss Boy with exclusive privileges that belonged to his position.

Two evenings later, there was a knock at my door. It was Mdala.

"Good evening, Sir. I have come to ask you a favour. Will it be possible for you to give the flat-boys a ride on your motorbike? That would make them very happy."

"What a good idea, Mdala. I would like you to organise a schedule for the boys and Tuesdays at 4 o'clock usually suits me. Discuss it with them and let me know so that we can coordinate our diaries. It is very considerate of you to consider the others."

"Thank you, Sir." Mdala was delighted. We understood each other and I had reinforced rather than undermined his position.

Six weeks later, all six of them had enjoyed a ride. Each passenger thanked me demonstratively with both hands together but their deepest gratitude they reserved for Mdala who had organised the exceptional treat for them.

I arrived home from lectures one evening a week later to find the supervisor of the flats, Mrs. van Niekerk, waiting for me in the corridor. She appeared to be dressed for a special occasion in a suit that must have been fashionable once. We had exchanged greetings but had never conversed before. Looking at her, I guessed she was about fifty years old. Her face, like the rest of her, was slim with few lines except along her forehead. Her hair was greying and she wore it pulled back into a roll at the nape of her neck. Behind her rimless spectacles, her brown eyes were clear and alert. Mrs. van Niekerk must have been an attractive woman when she was young.

"Mr. Sinclair, I wonder if I can speak to you in confidence on a private matter?" she asked quietly, her expression grave. I guessed something serious had happened.

"Certainly, Mrs. van Niekerk, do come in," I answered sympathetically as I unlocked the door.

Mrs. van Niekerk walked in ahead of me exuding a sense of proud ownership as she looked around the room. She sat down immediately and took a cigarette out of her handbag before placing the handbag at her feet thus giving the impression that her visit would not be of short duration. She lit the cigarette and inhaled deeply while I waited.

"The first cigarette of the day is the lekkerste," she said appreciatively. I never smoke during working hours." Mrs. van Niekerk spoke with an Afrikaans accent.

She looked around approvingly and then asked,

"What do you think of the furniture and curtains in your flat Mr. Sinclair?"

"Adequate." I answered.

"Now am I chuffed to hear *that!* I chose everything myself. When the tenants before you left I told the owner, Mr. Ledbetter - have you met Mr. Ledbetter?" I nodded.

"I told Mr. Ledbetter that it was high time for a change in here. He asked me to see to it. 'Do the best you can but don't be extravagant' was all he told me. I bought the furniture on Charley's red hot sale. Charley's Furniture only has one red hot sale a year so that was a lucky strike. I don't mean the cigarettes, Lucky Strike!" She laughed at her own humour.

"All the rest I got at OK Bazaars. I got the curtains at the Hub because if you buy your material there they make them up for nothing."

"Mr. Ledbetter must have been very pleased with your cost-saving."

"You're telling me. To show his thanks he gave me six tickets to Boswell's circus so that I could take my family. I haven't got a family and he should know that. I haven't got brothers or sisters you see so I took my ex husband between wives. He's just been re-divorced for the fourth time. You can't count on him; he can't stay the course not with me or anyone else. Ag, to be fair to the bum, women fall for him like a ton of bricks; big belly and all. He could never resist the attention.   I was his first wife and when he married me they wondered what he saw in me – 'how did you get him?' they asked. He stayed married to me for longer than any of the others. I've still got something they haven't got if I say so myself and that's why he comes back to me between wives like a bad penny that keeps turning up. But I stick to my guns - once bitten twice shy. 'Put *that* in your pipe and smoke it Stoffel van Niekerk,' I tell him. I sold the other four on the black market. Now don't get me wrong the black market hasn't anything to do with black people. Natives are not allowed to sit next to the whites you know." She hesitated and for her own reasons, raised her eyebrows and looked at me meaningfully before continuing,

"I sold the tickets for double what Mr. Ledbetter paid - *That's* the sort of black market I mean."

"Well done. May I offer you a drink Mrs. van Niekerk?"

"Ja, that would be nice, a beer please."

"Potato crisps?"

"No thanks."

"How about a few slices of biltong?"

"Now you're talking! I can never say no to biltong." I fetched both the beers and the biltong from the kitchen and wondered why she had come to see me.

"Cheers" she said as she raised her glass to mine, "Cheers," I answered and I sat down opposite her.

"Where's Wisdom?" she asked.

"He'll be in at six-thirty. He works flexible hours."

"That doesn't sound good to me. Not good at all. He should work all day. Don't stand any nonsense from him; they all play up if you give them half a chance."

"I'll do my best. You came here to speak to me in confidence Mrs. van Niekerk. How can I help you?" I asked prompting her to begin her confidential discussion.

"You can't help me, Mr. Sinclair. I have come to help *you!*" She looked around again with some satisfaction while giving her statement time to sink in. I waited while she drank a good deal of her beer between chewing bits of biltong.

"I have come to speak to you in confidence and I hope you will accept my advice in the spirit in which it is given." That didn't sound like her at all but rather like well-rehearsed words not of her own choosing.

"This is very interesting." I answered and indeed I wondered what help she had to offer.

"You have not been in our country long enough to know the ins and outs of our relationship with the natives and it is my duty to inform you. A number of people have brought to my notice their concern that you are far too familiar with the natives. Please do not take this the wrong way but I must tell you that if you give the natives a finger they will take a hand, you give them an inch and they take a yard," she recited from memory. Her rapid, monotonous tone was the give-away and suggested that if she stopped at any stage, she might loose the sequence.

"They are ungrateful creatures if you don't mind me calling a spade a spade. Soon they won't know their place." That sounded more like her. At that point she paused for either breath or effect, I couldn't tell which.

She took her time finishing her beer and I offered her another.

"Ja don't mind if I do." I got up, went to the kitchen and removed another cold beer from the O.K. Bazaars fridge - good old OK Bazaars. In the meantime Mrs. van Niekerk was looking about her with undisguised admiration.

"The main thing I have come to tell you is this; some people are hopping mad that you take the natives for rides on your motorbike, hopping mad let me tell you." Having dropped her bombshell, she looked at me expectantly clearly waiting for an explanation for my eccentric behaviour.

"So *that's* the problem. What is your advice Mrs. van Niekerk?"

"My advice is to not to be so boetie-boetie with the natives; not so boetie-boetie. It doesn't go down well with the people who have complained to me and not with other people either I can tell you. Take it from me, they skinner about you and I get the complaints."

"I'm sorry if that adds to your workload but I have never concerned myself with gossip and I think those people who have complained to you are overreacting."

"When they see you boetie-boetie with the natives by taking them for rides on your motorbike then make no mistake about it, they are not overreacting. They are *not* overacting!" she repeated in irritation. "It is my duty to deal with all complaints when it comes to people living in these flats." She stubbed out her cigarette giving the chore intense concentration as though it was the most important undertaking of the day.

"I often wonder how you people do things overseas because we have so many problems with people from overseas. Take my word for it South Africans have a gatvol. They are up to here," she said placing her hand under her eyes with her palm facing down. "I am talking now about the people who have complained to me. Do you understand?"

"I hear what you are saying but I don't understand your problem with overseas people. Apart from my giving rides to the cleaners, does my attitude bother *you* Mrs. van Niekerk?"

"It doesn't make any difference if it bothers me or it doesn't bother me. What I am telling you is that it bothers other people Mr. Sinclair and that's what counts. I can tell you it rubs them up the wrong way. I am just the go-between so to speak. Ja, that's me, the go-between and I take my job to heart. I don't pass the buck like some people do. I believe that honesty is the best policy. I've always believed that."

There was a short silence before she continued,

"I can tell you right now that university people from overseas with commie ideas have been sent packing right out of this country and back to where they came from, bundled onto the first plane. No questions asked. I tell you - no questions asked!"

"What do you think of people being bundled out of the country with no questions asked?"

"I don't mind telling you what I think. I say voetsek and good riddance to those people who come here and cause trouble, voetsek and good riddance. Now, I'm not saying that you are a commie Mr. Sinclair but I must warn you that people are skinnering."

"Whatever they say, I can assure you Mrs. Van Niekerk that communism is far from my political ideology and I do not intend to get involved in politics in any shape or form in this country."

"Well that's good to hear I must say. Straight from the horses mouth so to speak." Mrs. van Niekerk took another calming puff of her cigarette,

"In the beginning I never believed you were a commie but I must be honest with you, I began to wonder myself when you fell over yourself for the kaffirs. I like to be an open book about these things and I want to help you for your own good. For your own good! Ja, I want to help you over hurdles so that you don't land up in bladdy trouble. Does that make sense to you?"

"It makes a lot of sense and I'm grateful. Can you give me an example of what that bladdy trouble might be?"

"Hey?" she asked with a puzzled frown between her eyebrows so I rephrased my question.

"What sort of bladdy trouble could I land up in?"

"I can only say as I have just already told you that some overseas people have been deported, no questions asked. We don't want communists coming to South Africa and upsetting the apple cart. Do you know what I'm saying?

"Yes I know what you're saying. I find this conversation fascinating Mrs. van Niekerk. Who decides on who is to be deported?"

"The Government of course," she said with the air of one whose increasing irritation was in conflict with the pride she felt at being knowledgeable on such procedures.

"Then there must be informers. Does the government have informers do you think?"

She blinked rapidly, moistened her lips before taking the last gulp of beer. She carefully poked biltong from between her two front teeth and finally said,

"That is not for me to know. How can I know how the government gets its information? *Now tell me that!*" She was very indignant and her voice went up a decibel or two.

"My God, I have no idea how the government gets its information so it's no good looking to me. It's none of my besigheid." I guessed she meant that it was none of her business.

"I only know they get their information – they get their information and make no mistake about that! Word gets around you see. It gets around but don't go asking me how it gets around." Mrs. van Niekerk was worked up and she had become red in the face. I had the distinct feeling that the conversation was not going in the direction she had intended.

"I don't doubt it for one moment and I get the picture perfectly Mrs. van Niekerk. Thank you for your advice and I hope you will assure those people who have complained to you that I am not a commie and I have no intention of becoming one." I smiled thinking it best to keep things on a cordial footing at least from my side.

"And what about the motorbike rides then? Can I tell the people that have complained to me that you won't take kaffirs for rides on your motorbike anymore?" "I wouldn't dream of it if that makes me a commie with the threat of deportation hanging over my head!"

She half smiled. Mrs. van Niekerk was in no mood for a full smile. "You are lucky Mr. Sinclair to be living in this fantastic country after coming from your own cold, rainy place. I've never been overseas but I heard from Zoë's husband's cousin, Frikkie - Zoë's cousin-in-law you could say- that it rains *all* the time over there. 'If it's not snowing, it's raining and, it's *always* freezing cold,' he says. 'Take it from me, Gertie, you're not missing anything. Don't waste your money. Go to the Kruger instead' that's what he says and he means it all right. I have never been to the Kruger. Anyway, it would be a shame if you got deported back to that place. Frikkie says there's no place like South Africa."

"In that he's probably right," I agreed. As she made no move to leave, I picked up the glasses and carried them through to the kitchen. When I returned she leaned over for her handbag and stood up. She smoothed her skirt in much the same way as she might have smoothed ruffled feathers. She then reassured me that we had spoken in confidence "but that goes without saying," she added.

"Thank for your concern and for taking time to advise me." I said as I walked her to the door. She hesitated as though she had something important to say then thought better of it and said,

"You can come to me for advice at any time Mr. Sinclair, at any time. I must say you have put my mind at rest about being a commie. You can't blame me for thinking that like everybody else. No, you can't blame me for judging by what I saw."

"I don't blame you Mrs. van Niekerk. It cannot be easy to be in your position."

"Ja, you can say that again." Her attitude softened considerably. "You can't be too careful these days you know. People like me in responsible jobs have to try to help foreigners to understand our country before they give the natives the wrong ideas. I'm glad you understand that. We can't have commies coming here and thinking they know better. Overseas people have to learn how to treat the natives because they don't know it from birth like we do. They keep doing the wrong thing all the time." She shook her head, perplexed at the ignorance of overseas individuals and their commie ideas. She had calmed down and her high colour of a few minutes earlier had receded.

"When you're already grown-up it's hard to learn from scratch. That's what Sannie says. She says it's like teaching an old dog to do new tricks. Doesn't work she says. You have to be a South African to know how to treat the natives and to know how things work in this country. Ja, you have to be a South African! Sannie's clever all right. She knows a thing or two. You can rely on her for advice on anything."

"You are certainly doing your best to be helpful, Mrs. van Niekerk."

I took the liberty of giving her a pat on her back. She looked satisfied then as though she had succeeded in her mission after all.

"I like you Mr. Sinclair whatever they say and thanks for the beers."

As she made her exit, Mrs. van Niekerk took one last gratifying look around the room, put her hand out to shake mine and we wished each other a good night.

I would have passed off such a discussion as being of no more significance than that of a middle-aged woman trying to protect her lowly social position by keeping others less fortunate than her 'in their place.' I believed her fears were genuine and that her purpose was to preserve the only way of life she knew. However, I had an uncomfortable feeling that I was becoming entangled in a widening web of suspicion and that the 'help' I had been given was far more in the line of unpleasant, ill disguised threats bordering on moral blackmail. Mrs. van Niekerk seemed guileless but she was dedicated to her cause and she would be easily manipulated if she thought there was any danger of whites surrendering the privileges they enjoyed.

Was she carrying out instructions? Had she purposely seated herself in a specific chair so that I was bound to sit opposite her and I would therefore be in better view of a hidden camera and microphone? I had not been able to discover either camera or microphone in the flat but I somehow felt they were there. Was I becoming paranoid as I had suggested Mr. Patel was?

Mr. Patel had been quick to put two and two together. What would he have made of this? Initially, I had thought his inference that my every move was being watched, preposterous but all considered I was no longer so sure about that or anything.

Time, or the unfolding of events, would reveal the truth and in the meantime all I could do was to try to put such disagreeable thoughts to the back of my mind.

Nine

The phone rang. I answered in my usual way, "Sinclair.'

"Hello Roger, this is Barbara Deacon speaking. Perhaps you do not remember me but we have met in the canteen on one or two occasions. I work in the Arts Department." She sounded nervous.

"Of course I remember you Barbara." I answered surprised that she had reason to ring me.

"You must wonder why I'm phoning you; well it's about the university ball. The University holds an end of year ball and the organisers expect, quite rightly so, that staff members attend as well as the students. This poses a dilemma for me because I do not have a partner. I wonder if you have not already invited someone else, if you would like to be my partner that evening. I will quite understand if you have someone else in mind."

"To be honest Barbara, I have heard about the ball but hadn't seriously considered attending. Dancing has never been one of my social assets but if you are prepared to put up with my incompetent attempts then I shall be delighted to be your partner. Please let me know your address, the date and time I should be there to collect you and I'm sure we'll have a great evening."

"Thank you. This is such a relief. It is very difficult for women who do not have a 'steady' to attend functions at which partners are required. I find it embarrassing to have to initiate the invitation. I shall send the information to your office tomorrow morning. Good night Roger."

When I put the phone down, I thought how extraordinary it was that someone as attractive as Barbara would be without a boyfriend. She had perfect features, auburn hair, deep green eyes and pearly white teeth. If there was a drawback to her looks it was in my opinion, her lack of sparkle. On the few occasions I had seen her, she was either lost in her own thoughts or she wore a serious expression.

On reflection, was it really so extraordinary that she did not have a boyfriend? For each individual, man or woman, it is not a matter of having someone, but of having the right person. Meeting the right person was in the lap of the gods and it did not always lead to a happy-ending. Look at me, I reflected with a measure of self-pity. What did I ever do to deserve to fall in love with a person of the "wrong" colour and culture? God only knew I kept myself busy with new interests and social activities and yet whatever I did, a captivating, elusive, dark eyed beauty haunted my dreams.

The ball was a great success. Barbara was a delightful companion and she was beautiful in a bright emerald green dress that shimmered when she danced and made her eyes look even greener. I saw a charming side to Barbara that evening, she laughed and her eyes twinkled in an almost flirtatious manner as she enjoyed male attention to which I felt she was not normally accustomed.

We sat at a table with other staff members all of whom were in an appropriately light-hearted party mood. The ambience was friendly and relaxed no doubt due in large part to the band that played swinging music. Even I forgot that dancing was not my strongest point. When the band struck up a Paul Jones, we had the opportunity of changing partners frequently and danced with students who were transformed into Cinderellas of the night in their long dresses.

Amateur photographers kept themselves and their cameras busy; students keen no doubt to record their last momentous evening as university students.

I managed to wake up early the next morning to join the members of the club for our breakfast run and as everyone arrived, they called comments about the fabulous woman with whom I had been out the night before.

"Jeepers, you are a dark horse!" Andrew called to me, "where did you meet that doll? She's one to die for."

"What the hell are you all talking about?" I asked puzzled.

"Come off it you cannot deny that it was you in the picture with that glamour puss. Newspaper reporters can lie, but photographs? Not likely."

"I'm not denying anything, just haven't seen this morning's paper." I said truthfully. "It never arrives before I leave.'

"Hi Roger, who was that bird you were with last night?" Luigi had just arrived, "Some beauty and I should know!" I had no idea why he should know except that he was quite a handsome Italian and fancied his chances with the ladies.

Koen next, "Roger, you must tell me where you hang out. Where did you meet that drop-dead gorgeous chick? How do you do it man?"

"It takes personality!" I replied. I could not wait to see the morning paper.

When I saw the paper later I had to agree, the photograph on the Social page was a sensational picture of Barbara, and a good one of me too. It was the biggest picture on the page and the happiest. I could see why the fellows had ragged me.

I phoned Barbara, complimented her on the excellent picture and forgot all about it. Two days later, there was a letter from Alysha.

My dearest Roger

I saw that picture of you and a beautiful girl in the Sunday paper and got a dreadful shock. I nearly died of jealousy. Of course I know you are far too good looking, far too charming not to be involved in a social life but actually seeing evidence of it, was more painful than you can imagine. Why am I writing this? For two reasons; the first is because I feel upset and the second, for me any contact with you, however hopeless, however superficial, is better than no contact at all. Can you understand that Roger? I wonder.

My life goes on in a routine manner, one monotonous day after the other, with Ma and Pitajee growing more desperate in their efforts to find me a husband "before it's too late." I think they must know that it is already too late. Thank goodness, my two brothers are married with families so at least they are not making me feel guilty that they have no grandchildren. They love each other very dearly but they never fell in love as we did and therefore it is difficult for them to understand how I feel. Their idea is that a relationship of short duration can easily become a relationship of happy memories and then forgotten. I wish they were right!

Please write to me at the university. That way there will be less chance of unpleasant repercussions. I hope you still love me.

This goes with all my love from Alysha.

I suppose that under the circumstances I should not have been surprised to read how Alysha felt but I was disappointed that she did not trust me sufficiently to know that my going out with someone else had no bearing on my feelings for her. I answered her letter immediately.

My Beloved Alysha,

I was so pleased to hear from you although I was sorry to read that you were feeling jealous. How can you doubt that I love you? I fell in love with you at first sight, love you still and always will. Please never question that and if you find doubt creeping in simply because of our unenviable circumstances, think of those glorious days in England! Remember too "The Spotted Dog" that could not have been more exciting or more splendid had it been our wedding celebration and in a way it was. It was a magical day. I think of those things when I am alone and missing you dreadfully.

Barbara, the young woman in the photograph, invited me to go to the university ball with her because she didn't have a partner and I accepted since being on the staff, I too was expected to attend the function. I want to reassure you that there is no reason why you should be jealous of her or any other woman and by the way, I do not date other women!

Each day that passes brings my departure from South Africa a day closer. When my contract ends and I leave here, I know that we will be able to find a sanctuary, a country that suits both of us, a place where we can live together in peace and safety. We have to be patient my darling Alysha, it is not easy for you but it is not easy for me either. However, rest assured, the waiting will be worth it in the end!

Has you your father discussed the possibility of our going to India on holiday together? We need something to look forward to and to plan towards. By the way, I agree wholeheartedly with your father that extreme caution is necessary.

I feel threatened but I do not know where the danger lurks. Under no circumstances do I want you to be involved in any way should my fears prove to be well founded so please continue to keep our contact to an absolute minimum.

From your loving Roger.

Boetie phoned. He had also seen the newspaper photograph of course, who hadn't! Anyway, he said that the painting was finished and I could come and fetch it. I said I would be there on Saturday if that suited them.

"How much do I owe you?" I asked, as that had not seemed important until that moment.

"I normally sell only to galleries so I will charge you the same as I charge them. This way you will be getting a good price at two thousand rand and I won't be losing on the deal."

Two thousand rand!

When I saw the painting I forgot the price. What a moment to remember. We were in Boetie's studio when he pulled aside a sheet to reveal the most wonderful rural painting I had ever seen. It was very large, 150cm x 75cm; a most brilliant work of art that fully engaged the senses of beauty, wonder, happiness and recognition. Nostalgia would come later. It would require and demand its own wall, its own space. I could hardly drag myself away from what I was certain was Boetie's masterpiece.

Boetie was pleased with my generous and sincere compliments while I wondered how he could possibly part with so fine a work of art.

He had painted a kraal scene with traditional huts, fever trees, flowering aloes, indigenous shrubs and vegetation that captured the atmosphere and sensations of Africa. Wisdom, while being the focal point, did not dominate the painting. It was such a good likeness to him that it was hard to believe Boetie had never met my right hand man. The painting was immediately my most aesthetic, precious possession and I knew it would always be. I decided to ship it straight to England. Before doing so, I had it professionally photographed and I gave a smaller, framed copy to Wisdom. When he saw it, Wisdom jumped high into the air as though his legs were made of springs.

Marion and Frank Guthrie had invited me to spend the day with them on the next Sunday so I decided to accept their invitation and forgo my usual breakfast run. I had not seen them since we met in Muizenberg.

Sunday morning was chilly and very misty when I set off to Nottingham Road. I found the Guthrie's home quite easily because their stud farm was well signposted from the main road. I arrived to large, imposing wrought iron gates and pressed a button at the entrance. I spoke into the intercom and Frank opened the gates by remote control. Frank was certainly up to date with the latest security inventions. I drove up the driveway to an impressive, sprawling ranch style house.

After morning tea with Marion and Frank, he asked me if I would like to see his horses. I accepted the invitation readily and welcomed the opportunity to walk in the hilly countryside. Shrouded in mist and mystery, the undulations reminded me of the South Downs of England. The moist, gentle weather was a pleasant change from the usual sunny days.

The property was vast and it boasted a racetrack that Frank told me was for exercising and training the horses. He had a team of excellent black employees who were first-class riders. They exercised the horses and groomed them, cleaned the stables and were indispensable to the successful running of his business.

Frank then took me to the stables. It was spring and the foaling season. It was a special experience for me to see so many horses with their ponies in the paddock and then mares with their foals in the stables. One of the foals had been born only a few hours previously and it was already standing on its spindly little legs. I had never questioned my decision to be a physicist but I could well imagine swapping my career for this delightful, rural lifestyle.

It crossed my mind that they must have done very well out of the sale of their tobacco farm!

"Marion, have you settled down or do you still miss your life in Rhodesia?" I asked during lunch.

"I miss it terribly. I loathe the politics here particularly the apartheid system after the relaxed existence we all took for granted in Rhodesia. When I think of the easy-going rapport we farmers enjoyed with our farm labourers and how contented our black people were when compared with what goes on here, I feel miserable. You have no idea what upsetting racial incidents I have seen and read of. Everyone in Rhodesia, regardless of colour, had an opportunity in life even if he or she were not able to take advantage of it. There were no laws to prevent their advancement. Well, there is just no comparison between the two countries and I find the attitudes here detestable."

"Have you made any friends in the neighbourhood?" I asked her.

"I'm beginning to make friends and that makes a difference to my social life of course. I have joined the Women's Institute and go to their meetings once a month. The trouble is that South African women and I think so differently. I try not to criticise the injustices I see all around me but that is not easy. It doesn't help that Frank and I miss our daughters. They are at St. Anne's in Hilton and as it is one of the best private schools and not too far from here, we feel we cannot complain in that respect. Fortunately, the girls are very happy there."

"From what I have heard, you cannot get better than St. Anne's. It is famous far beyond the borders of South Africa."

"Yes, we booked them in before we left Rhodesia."

I left at four o'clock in the afternoon after an interesting visit and the pleasure of walking in the misty hills. They invited me to visit them "at any time" and I decided to do that when the girls were home on holiday and Marion would be feeling more cheerful.

Frank walked with me to my car and said,

"You must have noticed Marion's depression. She is finding it very difficult to snap out of it. The doctor prescribed anti-depressants but her mood swings were extreme and that was no good either so she's battling it out. The situation in South Africa is far from perfect but the world she misses is fast disappearing and she has to accept that just as she has to accept the fact that our new lifestyle away from family, friends and familiar places is what most Rhodesians will be facing now or in the near future. We cannot go back and would not choose to do so but homesickness is not dependent on, or cured by, good common sense!"

"I did notice Frank and I hope she will get over it soon. I think that when she becomes involved with the horses, she will start recovering. Encourage her to take an interest in the mares with their foals. That should do the trick. Good luck Frank, see you soon." I decided to mention her to Annabel in case they had not already met at the Women's Institute.

I drove away thinking how fortunate Marion was and she didn't know it. But then in fairness to Marion, she was measuring her happiness and her sense of justice by a different yardstick and could not close her eyes to what was going on around her. She had compassion for her fellow human beings and her impotence to do anything about that, her inability to accept the status quo was causing her mental anguish. Those factors made her homesickness more wretched and in that frame of mind, nothing was right. To be able to live in South Africa, one had to have the ability to "switch off" or go nuts. I was fast discovering that for myself.

If Alysha and I could be married and live together without fear of the consequences and in that house, we would think that heaven had come to earth. It was obviously an unrealistic comparison because as long as apartheid and its iniquities existed, our situation and our idea of happiness could not be compared with anyone else's.

Ten

I had not had much contact with Alysha in weeks. How awful it was to be wary of phoning because our phones were probably tapped, wary of writing because our letters may be intercepted and under no circumstances to be seen together so when I received a letter from her, it took me by surprise. Although it was a pleasant surprise, I became painfully aware of the fact that I was living in two worlds. There was the exterior world of apartheid to which I appeared to adhere and that was a very comfortable world of privilege and wellbeing. Then there was my inner world of secrecy and, to a certain extent, hypocrisy. The people I associated with would never have guessed nor understood that I loved a woman of a different race. I felt a cheat not being true to my friends and nor to myself so that the emotional conflict of duplicity that I lived with, took its toll of my peace of mind. I was not able to shut Alysha out of my heart, not out of my thoughts and certainly not out of my life whatever the laws of the land might legislate. I was committed to a contract in South Africa and was bound to the country for a definite period so I had to live the life of a white South African. I was torn between my two worlds and I felt resentful that love and something as insignificant as the colour of my skin could make me act out a life of deception. I opened the letter.

Alysha wrote that as I had made all the arrangements for England because it was my country and I knew it well, would I like her to put together an itinerary for India? *What a question!* I didn't mind where we went or what we saw. The prospect of being with her day and night was the only thing that mattered. We could go to Timbuktu for all I cared.

We made our separate bookings. I flew to London a week in advance of Alysha's departure and went to see my family in Devon. It was a year since I had last seen them. My father and my brothers and families told me they had all taken to Alysha immediately and my young nephews were infatuated with her.

"And, how did you feel Mum?" I asked knowing she would give me an honest answer.

"I didn't empathize with her immediately because we come from different cultural worlds but that will come. A weekend was not long enough for us to get to know each other. For example, I did not know whether she liked our food because I believe Indians eat mainly curry and rice dishes. I could have asked her but that wouldn't have helped if she had not liked it because I have no knowledge of eastern cookery. Little things like that worried me. They were trifling details and in retrospect unimportant. What I want above all else, is that you find happiness in marriage as your brothers have done. If Alysha makes you happy, I will love her."

I was pleased to hear that. Funny how a mother's positive opinion is such matters can make one feel so good.

My family members were dismayed when they heard of the risks we ran in seeing each other. My brothers were inclined to think I was exaggerating the facts but Dad was concerned,

"My advice to you is – Get out of the place! Break your contract in South Africa as soon as possible and find a country, perhaps the United States, where you and Alysha can live in safety. There too you will be able to pursue your career ambitions. South Africa is notorious for its apartheid policy and you are taking grave risks."

"I cannot break my contract without unpleasant repercussions quite apart from the fact that I have a moral obligation towards the students. My contract ends in six months time and, in all honesty, it will not difficult to last the course. I have made a life for myself and I love the endless space, the climate and the Drakensberg Mountains that lie within a couple of hours drive from where I live. It is a wonderful country and I have made a circle of friends from many walks of South African life. Alysha and I have already considered the United States and I have begun looking into career opportunities there. Please, Dad, do not worry about me. Alysha and I take no chances and under the circumstances, we see very little of each other."

Mum too asked me to be careful, wished me a happy holiday in India and sent "her love to Alysha."

I could have sung my happiness from the rooftops as my plane landed at Delhi Airport! There was the same confusion as three or four years before and when I finally had my luggage, I was one of the lucky ones – many suitcases could not be found. The officials blamed Heathrow but my guess was that the missing cases lay buried under piles of luggage from other flights.

I saw Alysha immediately. She seemed to stand out in the crowd but if that was possible, I wonder! She was dressed like all the other Indian women and yet to my eyes she was exceptional. We had not seen each other for so long that in our excitement, we both talked at the same time and then lapsed into simultaneous silence. Then we laughed, relaxed and settled down finally to accepting our joy at being together.

"Darling," she said using that term of endearment in words for the first time "I thought it would be a good idea to spend tonight in Delhi and then leave for Jaipur tomorrow morning. Jaipur is one of my favourite places and I am so looking forward to showing you around. I hope you agree that it would be best to see Rajasthan properly rather than rush around trying to see as much of the country as possible."

"Just being together is what it's all about so we'll enjoy any place on earth but if Jaipur is your favourite, then it must be special." I answered as I hugged her.

"Oh by the way, we don't want to think of home yet but Goofy and Mira will be going to Mauritius for a short break when we get back and they've asked me if I'll stay in their house, feed the dogs, etc. Goofy suggested that we could spend that weekend with them. Our flight lands in the evening when it will be dark. Goofy will meet me/us at the airport and then on Sunday evening he could drop you off at the Westville Hotel. Wisdom should fetch you from there. They love Mauritius and will be there for a week leaving on the Monday morning."

"That's a great idea."

Alysha and I set off to Jaipur by taxi the next morning. It was not our first experience of the traffic and yet we were just as appalled by it as we had been on our visit to Agra a few years earlier.

Fortunately, we arrived in Jaipur without mishap though that was more a matter of good luck than good driving skill on behalf of our chauffeur.

Alysha told me as much as she could about Jaipur, The Pink City, so called because the buildings were built of pink sandstone. Jaipur, the capital of Rajasthan, had a rich and exciting history due mainly to the exceptional Maharajas who had ruled the state for two and a half centuries. Alysha knew the ins and outs of all the places we visited and during the course of our stay, we must have seen every temple, palace, fort and courtyard for miles around! The most remarkable was the Jal Mahal palace built in the middle of a lake. Its mystical beauty and serenity became imprinted in my memory so that the scene with hills in the background and its reflection on the water would come to mind whenever I thought of India.

Most of the historical buildings were national monuments. Monkeys scampered around them while elephants carried local people for rides; a sad comedown for them after the pomp and ceremony of their glorious past.

We stayed in Rambagh Palace that had been the home of all the Maharajas of Rajasthan and had recently been converted into a hotel with its original furniture, oriental carpets, hunting trophies and relics of former times still in place.

"Don't you just love this place!" Alysha exclaimed at the end of our first day in Jaipur. "I feel honoured to be here enjoying the stately beauty of the palace, to be experiencing the splendour and grandeur of a bygone era that existed until recently. Roger, do you also feel the wonder and joy of the regal atmosphere, the world of Indian magic and luxury?" Her exuberance and pleasure were inexhaustible.

The hotel was indeed impressive. I found Indian culture to be interesting and vastly different from that of my own sober western world but for Alysha it went deeper than that. She was in her element, euphoric at being in the country of her roots with its familiar traditions and customs. She belonged.

Before dinner, we went into the lounge where photographs on the walls lent a homely touch to the elegance of the room and for a short while we lost ourselves in Jaipur's illustrious past.

There were personal photographs in the drawing room that provided the viewer with a visual tour of historical interest. They depicted the Maharajas' weddings, the ornate and costly gold lame costumes and turbans they wore, the extravagance of their entourages and the procession of elaborately dressed and jewel-bedecked elephants. It had been a world of unimagined luxury and opulence. There were photographs of other state occasions through the years and all were equally majestic.

Then on a different wall, were photographs of famous visitors one being of the Maharaja and his wife with Queen Elizabeth and Prince Philip at the palace in 1963. Amongst the other famous visitors was Jackie Kennedy, wife of the President of the United States. She was an elegant woman but pictured next to the fragile beauty of the Maharani, even she looked gauche.

There were polo photographs of the Maharaja and Prince Philip's teams playing against each other both in England and in Jaipur. It was hard to believe that it had all gone for good and yet harder to believe, that such a life had ever existed.

One late afternoon as we sat relaxing in the peaceful surroundings, we saw a graceful woman dressed in a white sari, walk across the lawn. Two gardeners were trimming a hedge at the time and when they saw her, they immediately left what they were doing and, one after the other they knelt down and touched her feet.

Alysha was very excited, "She is the Maharani of Jaipur, the wife of the last Maharaja! She lives in a home in the grounds. I know so much about her, Roger. I have read the autobiography she wrote and it is a marvellous personal story of great historic value. She was such an exceptional woman and for years, she made all the lists of the ten most beautiful women in the world. She had such an exotic, exciting life that combined the best of both worlds, eastern and western. It must be very sad for her to see this wonderful palace, her former home with all its memories and its long family history, occupied by strangers who come and go on a regular basis. The country should never have got rid of the Maharajas when it gained independence!"

"I disagree with you on that point. There were 800 Maharajas in India and most of them were spoilt, self-indulgent tyrannical rulers concerned only with the vulgarities of splendour and their own extravagant comfort while the people in their States lived in poverty. The Maharajas who ruled Jaipur, were exceptions. They formed an incomparable dynasty and were much loved by the people but I don't think the vast majority of ruling families were mourned at all when the system ended."

"The country would have been far better off if as much effort had been put into ending the caste system as was put into ridding the country of its ruling families,"

Alysha said with conviction.

"I don't think it should have been a question of either or, but of both. With the partitioning of India, life changed profoundly on this continent."

Alysha agreed with me but she viewed the pomp and ceremony that surrounded the ruling families with a romantic eye.

When our holiday ended, we felt disheartened at the prospect of yet another separation for perhaps months, but we also felt more optimistic that we had agreed on positive plans for our future. On our return to South Africa and with the end of my contract well in sight, I would apply for a position in the United States. If I were successful then Alysha would do the same. That we hoped would be where we could build a life and a future together.

Eleven

Alysha and I endured a long and tiring return journey flying first by Indian Airways to Mauritius and then by South African Airways to Johannesburg from where we got a connecting flight to Durban.   Goofy was at the airport to meet us but he gave no sign of recognition when he saw me and nor I of him. He helped Alysha with her luggage and they left the building headed I presumed to the parking area. I took an overly long time to collect my luggage. I bought a newspaper and then I too went through the exit. The timing was perfect because at that moment, I saw Goofy's car approaching. It was after sunset, dark outside and the lighting was poor so at first, it was impossible to read the number plate but it was Goofy all right. The car stopped, I opened the back door, put my case on the back seat and then climbed in. No one followed us. Whew. So far so good!

Rush hour had passed so the road was virtually empty and it was not long before we arrived in Reservoir Hills.

We did not suffer from jet lag between India and South Africa, so Alysha and I were not tired and after dinner the four of sat for hours exchanging news of South African events and our holiday. There was much to hear about South Africa since there was always something going on particularly in the political arena and seldom was it good news. Finally, we all went to bed and, speaking for myself, fell into a deep sleep.

It must have been about four o'clock in the morning when we were all awoken by loud banging on the front door and the dogs barking ferociously. The lights in the house went on so I realised Goofy must have got up to investigate. I jumped out of bed to join him and saw Goofy with a gun in his hand. He called to Mira and Alysha to stay where they were. Mira in a shaky voice said that she was phoning the police and no on was to open the door.

A police van arrived to join the one that, unbeknown to us, was already in the driveway. Goofy opened the door and two police officers entered the house and grabbed hold of me handcuffing my hands behind my back.

"Are you Mr. Roger Sinclair?" The taller of the two officers demanded to know of me.

"Yes, I am."

"You are under arrest. You must be made aware of your rights and anything you say may be held in evidence against you," he said – or words to that effect. I was shocked. I could hardly take in what was happening or what anyone was saying.

Alysha and Mira came through to the hall where we were standing, Mira was protesting and Alysha was in tears. Alysha tried to put her arms around me but one of the officers gently pulled her away. He seemed reluctant to do so which seemed odd considering that in his job it would hardly have been an unusual procedure. He then asked Goofy to bring my shoes and told me to put them on.

The next thing I was aware of was being led outside into the darkness of the night where the only brightness was provided by the blinding, flashing searchlights of the police vans. There was something unnerving about the surreal scene.

The sinister, unspoken fear of discovery that we had endured for many months, had become reality.

The police officers climbed into the front of the van and drove off. I sat in the dark at the back of the van and without a proper seat; I almost lost my balance every time the vehicle took a bend. I think I was too dazed and shocked by the unexpected events to have any particular thoughts during the journey but I did wonder about the other suspects who had sat there before me, no doubt some were criminals while perhaps others had done very little to fall foul of the law. All would have been treated as I was as proven criminals; poor buggers. The van stopped so I guessed we had finally reached our destination. I had never known the road from Reservoir Hills to Maritzburg, if that was where we were, to take so long.

Once inside the police station, an official whose expression was one of undisguised contempt when he read out the charge against me – contravention of the Immorality Act - asked me whether I had anything to say.

I told him that I had not.

A Prison guard lead me through to a single cell where I was to spend the night, what was left of it. The room was bare except for a bed, a blanket, a thin pillow, a small table and a chair. He closed the heavy metal door behind him and I was alone. I almost smiled at the incongruity of the contrast with Rambagh Palace Hotel; was it really only two nights ago? My tentative smile faded before it materialized; the horrible truth was that I, Roger Sinclair, was in jail!

That night and the nights that followed were the most uncomfortable of my entire life. A light glowed in my cell the whole night through and I could not find a switch to put if off. Searching for a light-switch took a matter of seconds since the walls were bare. I would have thrown my shoe at the light-bulb to shatter it but it was encased in firm metal netting that was attached to the ceiling. The atmosphere was so dry that my eyes stung and my throat hurt. I guessed there was some sinister reason for the condition of the cells and that it was a way of reducing prisoners to psychological wrecks. Well, I decided, that would not happen to me.

There was something to be said for knowing the worst and facing up to it. I had lived for so long with uncertainty of all that could happen and now that it had happened, I was determined to be strong-minded and to endure whatever lay ahead. I might waver but I would not give in.

The following morning, breakfast was mealie meal porridge and a lukewarm drink that might have been tea or coffee, I could not distinguish the difference. A prison official visited me to tell me that my lawyer had made an appointment to see me at two o'clock on Monday afternoon. I did not know that I had a lawyer so that was rather interesting. I guessed the authorities would not release me before that meeting so I resigned myself to incarceration for the next few days at least. I asked whether I could have a copy of either the Witness or The Natal Mercury.

"You will have to pay for it," the guard said.

"I was brought here without clothing or money so will you please tell me how I can possibly pay for a newspaper?" I was still wearing my pyjamas.

"You will be charged for it at the end of your stay."

Well that was a way of putting it: my stay!

He left without a word and returned with The Natal Mercury.

Spread across the front page of the newspaper in huge bold black letters, were the words, "Natal University Professor arrested for contravention of the Immorality Act." The article carried my full name, my age and my nationality along with my picture. The picture was part of the photograph taken with Barbara at the students' ball. The article stated that the charge was "consorting with an Asian woman."

I was grateful that the press had not stated Alysha's name particularly as the article insinuated that the Asian woman was a prostitute. I was outraged being defenceless against such slander.

An hour later, the same guard who had delivered the newspaper, brought my suitcase and told me that I had permission to dress in my own clothes. I had not been in anyone else's clothes I assured him. His expression did not change. He then removed my suitcase from the cell. The alternative I suppose would have been prison garb.

The same guard who was the only person I saw that morning, delivered lunch to my cell. Not only was the bread and jam singularly unappetising, but I had no desire for food of any description.

Sunday was a repetition of Saturday. I was able to buy the Sunday papers and much to my dismay, they carried even more publicity than had the papers on Saturday! To all intents and purposes, the media had accused, tried and found me guilty of one of South Africa's most shameful crimes without there ever having been a formal hearing.

At exactly two o'clock on Monday afternoon, a different police attendant entered the cell and told me that my lawyer had arrived. He brought an extra chair into the room.

"How do you do Mr. Sinclair, I am Max Feinstein."

"How do you do," I responded as we shook hands.

The guard left us alone and shut the cell door behind him. Mr. Feinstein and I sat opposite each other at the little table. We observed each other. He was a tall man with a kindly face and white hair. He had a direct and honest gaze and I liked that about him. He was very businesslike in his approach.

"Mr Feinstein how is it that you are my lawyer and I know nothing about you? Have you been appointed by the Court?" That being the case, fat chance I had.

"No. Mr. Patel telephoned me very early yesterday morning, told me the story and asked me if I would represent you."

"That was very considerate of Mr. Patel. I appreciate his assistance because I would not know where to begin to find a lawyer who would be prepared to take on what appears to be a hopeless case. Are you prepared to take it on Mr. Feinstein? I know that advocates hate losing cases and this one appears to be lost already!"

"Mr. Sinclair…"

I interrupted him,

"Please call me Roger, its less formal particularly under the circumstances,"

"Roger, if I take on this case, it will have far more far-reaching consequences than you or the government can imagine at this point. Let me explain. If you plead guilty, and you do not need me for that, you will be fined and deported from the country and the identity of the young woman in question will not be revealed. Apart from your reputation that will be in shreds, damage will be zilch. Since you are not a South African, your reputation, particularly due of the nature of the crime, may be of no consequence to you.

What has the government to gain by victimising you and making the most of this situation, you may ask? They have much to gain. You see every case that is publicised is a lesson to others."

"What else can I do other than plead guilty and get the hell out of here?"

"You can plead 'not guilty' and do a great service to this country and to those people whose lives and reputations have been destroyed by the exploitation of the Immorality Act. Because of the social class you and Miss Patel belong to and your educational achievements, you can be of great assistance to the anti-apartheid movement by allowing them to expose the bizarre ideologies of Apartheid."

"That would then mean a court case and extra publicity, no doubt negative. I do not see how that could help anybody."

"You are a British physicist who apparently had an affair; maybe even fell in love with an Indian physicist. She was not just any Indian woman of easy virtue whom you slept with for brief pleasure as has been implied in the press. Her father is a leading business executive of international repute. Her family is highly respected in the Indian community both here and abroad. There is a strong anti-apartheid movement outside our country and it has been waiting for a case that will capture the public's imagination and involve them emotionally in the ramifications of the Immorality Act. This is a dream scenario."

"The anti-apartheid movement has its noble cause but how would the Patel family feel about Alysha being exposed to adverse publicity in this way?"

"Please bear in mind that Mr. Patel has engaged me!"

How would Alysha take it I wondered? I knew she would be devastated that I was in prison, that our love for each other had been so publicly degraded. Would the stress be so great, that she would regret ever having met me? Could things ever be the same again? I mulled over negative assumptions. I decided that, knowing Alysha as I did, she would far rather that I stood up for our love than slink away a beaten man. My fighting spirit, one that I had seldom been aware of or needed, surfaced and I said,

"Max, we'll go for it!"

"I'm pleased. You will need stamina, courage and a strong heart and do not forget that you will be found 'guilty as charged.' The laws of apartheid must be seen to be upheld by the courts so no exceptions can be made. They cannot go soft on this."

"I'm fit. I've just returned from holiday and feel that I can take on the world."

We shook hands.

At 2 o'clock on Tuesday afternoon, I was released on bail of five thousand rand, I had been required to surrender my passport and I was to report to the police every day. Max informed me that an anonymous donor had stood bail. The only person I could think of was Mr. Patel but I did not ask who it was.

When I left prison, my case in hand, I knew how a criminal must feel carrying his pathetic worldly possessions on his way to face a hostile world. It was a desolate feeling. The euphoria of my discussion with Max evaporated and I felt isolated and alone.

As I walked to the main gates, I heard someone call,

"Hey Roger, come this way!"

It was Boetie! I had never felt as pleased to see a friend as I did at that moment.

"Don't tell me," he said as he gave me a bear hug. "I know you've been through hell. I'm taking you home with me. Annabel is worried and wants to care for you."

"Can't come. I have to report to the police at ten o'clock every day."

"I've arranged for you to report to the police in Nottingham Road." I experienced a tremendous sense of gratitude and my blood that had run cold for days causing me to shiver at odd moments, warmed miraculously.

"Do you mind if we go to the flat first? I want to check on Wisdom. I haven't seen him since my return."

"No problem. I'll drop you off and then pick you up in half an hour later. I must collect some paints."

I knocked at the front door and Wisdom opened it.

"Haw Sir," he said. "The police came on Saturday morning and they pulled out all the files; papers everywhere. I have been working all this time trying to put everything back in place. Not finished yet. I do not know what they were looking for. They did not ask me to help them to find it. Did you have a good holiday, Sir?"

"Yes thank you Wisdom I had a good holiday."

"Some post came this morning. I have put it in separate piles."

I glanced at the small piles of letters, one he had labelled "hate mail" another "friendly mail." There were a few unopened envelopes; letters he thought were private correspondence. I stuffed those into a plastic bag that I would take with me. I repacked my case with clean clothing while Wisdom made a pot of tea.

Wisdom was highly nervous. I could tell that by his rapid speech and his solemn expression.

"Sir, Mdala and the flat boys said I must tell you they send you their greetings. Their hearts bleed for you. Mine does too, Sir."

Not having seen him for a while, I realised how very young and vulnerable he was. Too young for what was going on around him.

"Please thank them Wisdom and don't you worry about me."

I told Wisdom that I would be going away for a few days. I would phone him regularly and I gave him money for any unforeseen expenses. I also wrote down Boetie's phone number so that he could contact me if necessary.

"Be careful, please Sir."

"I'll do my best."

I decided to drive myself so that I could report to the police every day and free to leave when I wanted to without inconveniencing Boetie.

I arrived at the house before Boetie did. Annabel came out to the car. She put her arms around me and kissed me in a maternal way as my mother might have done then she showed me to a bedroom and suggested that I unpack and settle in. It didn't take me long to unpack. I took out the envelopes from the plastic bag and opened the first one.

Dear Roger,

I wonder if you can imagine how horrified we all were to read the shocking, screaming headlines that appeared in all the national newspapers. It was worse for those of us who thought we knew you than for those who read the story purely for sensationalism because we, your friends, did not have a clue as to what was going on in your life. When you arrived from England, you knew nothing of the South African culture or the laws of our country. With Elaine's help and mine, and that of others, you learned fast. You were therefore well aware of our Apartheid laws and the Immorality Act though none of us thought there was the remotest chance that you would contravene them. As we often told you, the laws of this country were designed for very sane reasons and for the well-being of all its citizens.

Our disappointment is all the more painful because we adopted you and took you into our homes and lives. We made sure you met delightful young women any one of whom would have made a most suitable companion and/or wife and we feel let down. You have let your friends down; you have let your university down and above all, you have let yourself down.

We recognize that what has been done cannot be undone. However, sincere friendship and affection survives the frailties of man and forgives so having said all of the above, Elaine and I want to wish you all the best for what will be a very trying and painful court case. We hope when it is all over that you will be able to put this nightmare behind you and that you will remember, just as we do, the good times we have enjoyed together, the happy times.

Whatever anyone might think right now, we will all miss you, your sense of humour and your intelligent opinions on a wide variety of subjects.

Till we meet again hopefully under better circumstances,

I remain your friend,
Nigel.

That sounded like Nigel all right when he got on his high horse, sanctimonious and lecturing. It struck me as being the sort of admonishment that a man would give his wayward son and that Nigel had taken that liberty in the name of our friendship to do just that. I opened the next letter without any expectation of its contents and saw that it was from Jeremy.

My dear Roger,

Words fail me, as does my imagination when it comes to what you must be going through right now. Sally and I feel devastated at this tragic turn of events. I feel sorry that you did not confide in us but what could we have done other than to advise you most seriously not to go down that path. You are not one of us in the sense that you were not born and brought up in this country with our unique national laws, laws ingrained into us from birth, laws of so-called immorality. Therefore, we feel desperately sorry for you and for what has happened to you.

The woman whoever she might be must be a very special person of intelligence or you would not have had an affair with her and consequently become a victim of our inflexible laws.

If we can do anything at all to help you, please let us know. I cannot think of what we can do, but should there be anything, please do not hesitate to call on us. We are here for you.

I will keep in touch with you and visit you if that is possible. Being inexperienced with this type of thing, not knowing what is and what is not allowed, I shall make enquiries of the authorities.

Sally sends her best wishes and please rest assured that we are thinking of you, praying for you and we think no less of you!

Good luck with the court case. Wish I could advise you but I cannot. I hope you have a good defence lawyer.

Best regards,
Jeremy.

I appreciated Jeremy's support and his willingness to assist if he could. I took my time before opening the next letter considering whether I wanted to do so or not. I was in no mood to be patronised or reproached by friends in the personal matter of whom I loved and who I slept with.

My dear Roger,

I feel very upset about the headline news of you in our papers. The reason why I feel emotionally involved is that I love you! I had so hoped you might in time return my love and until now, I had not given up hope that that might happen. One of my happiest and most memorable evenings was the night of the end-of-year ball when we were partners. I would never have confessed my love for you except under these extreme circumstances when I have nothing to gain or lose by doing so. Our courts will put you through the mill and I want you to know that you have many supporters, people like me who admire you for the person you are and many others who have political interests and feel that our country has lost its senses. I send you my heartfelt good wishes for the best possible outcome.

Sincerely,
Barbara.

I had no idea that Barbara felt that way about me and I was sorry for her. I knew how miserable love could be. Love had got me into this 'ruddy' fix! I decided not to read any more letters from friends or acquaintances until I noticed that there was one from the Harley Davidson club.

Roger,

Our club members never question one another in important matters and we don't pass judgement. There are only two certainties to the tight spot you are in. One is that you will be deported and the other is that we will miss you. Our Sunday mornings will not be the same without your typically Pommie brand of humour! From the beginning, you have been one of us in spirit and friendship and now in your time of trouble, we are

100 percent with you. We will follow the case closely when it starts and rest assured that if we can support you in any way, we will be there in force to do so!

Your friends of the Harley Davidson Club.

Every club member had signed the letter. There were few rules to membership of the club but a strict code of honour prevailed. Brotherhood was important and support was only withdrawn from a member in cases of rape, murder, violence, burglary or any other crime harmful to others. There had never in the history of the Pietermaritzburg Club been a member of such low moral calibre.

I decided that I might as well read the last two letters as well.

Roger,

You idiot! You kept to the rules of the game on board ship; you should have kept to the rules of the game on terra firma too! If it's any consolation to you, you are not the only idiot in town. I made a blunder *big time* when I married Magda.

"It was love at first sight," she cooed soon after we met; she thought my job as chief game warden was 'marcho' and most 'romaarntic' - until she found that she hated the bushveld. She went on safari once and vowed never again! She made no secret of the fact that animals in the wild were "Dull as deesh water. I've seen them all in de zoo."

Magda was a knock-out as you know and all heads turned when she walked by. That overawed me and made me feel very proud in the beginning but I was soon bored to tears by her and her beauty. Never more so than on the boat when her only interest was to lie in the sun from mid morning when she woke up until sunset. She was not in the mood for any night-time activity either; she had to be fresh to catch a tan again the next day.

A few months after 'arriving at' our home (I cannot say 'settling in' because Magda never settled), a wealthy American wildlife photographer, cigar-chewing, loud, fat and twice her age, swept her off her feet and out of my life. That was not the bad part; the bad part was that it cost me an arm and a leg. I had to pay alimony for a year until he married her a month ago. I should have sued him for Alienation of Affection but I was scared to death he might change his mind! That's the story of my life. Now I read that you are in the thick of things.

If you have the time and inclination when this publicity stunt ends, please come to the Kruger as my guest. Two of the chaps on the staff play bridge and we are always on the lookout for a fourth. It is a unique treat in the evenings to play under the stars with our primitive lighting system and the incredible noises of the night, the shrieks and growls of animals hunting or being hunted – a fantastic experience that you should not miss.

Write when you have time. I send my best wishes and Good Luck with the case. I will be holding thumbs for you.

Best regards,
Graham.

I smiled at that letter. It was all about his problems and not mine and that was a pleasant change. Had things been different, I would have jumped at the opportunity to visit him because unlike Magda, I loved the bushveld. I had been to Hluhluwe and Mkuze game reserves in Zululand but only in mid summer when the game was difficult to spot because when there was enough water, the animals were not reliant on the waterholes. However, after much searching the guide pointed out springbok, giraffes, zebras and a rhino too quite close by and that was rewarding. They were all well camouflaged and only an experienced eye could have detected them.

Then to the last letter:

Dear Professor Sinclair,

I hereby inform you of the outcome of a special Board meeting of the Educational Department at which the Board debated the negative publicity given to you in the national press. The Board concluded that it is in your best interests and in the best interests of universities at which you lecture throughout the country, that you be put on non active service as from to-day's date. Your remuneration will continue until your contract ends.

We wish to acknowledge, and to thank you for your outstanding contribution to the Physics department and the academic benefits derived by the students.

I am to pass on to you the sympathy of the Board and the Board's best wishes that this dark period will soon pass.

Yours sincerely,

The letter was signed by the President of the Board.

I was satisfied with the contents of the letter. I lay down and must have fallen asleep immediately. It was the first deep and peaceful sleep I had had since Rambagh Palace a lifetime ago. I slept until the next morning!

I dressed and went outside feeling a different person and so much more optimistic. It was early and no one else was about. The morning was fresh and crisp. How I would miss the clear, sparkling mornings in Africa! Where in the world could anyone find anything quite like this?

After breakfast, I told Annabel and Boetie the full story of Alysha starting with our meeting in Delhi almost four years previously. I also told them that, ludicrous as it seemed, I had decided to plead "Not guilty."

"Well, why not? It makes no difference how you plead you are in blerrie trouble right up to your eyebrows. The main thing is that you don't end up in the clink." Boetie's comment was hardly cheering! "I know of much worse situations than yours. Eventually, people who refuse to cooperate with the government find themselves manoeuvred into embarrassing situations and then blackmailed in the name of this damned Act. It is one of the most abused of all laws.

For example, a top business executive in Johannesburg, not helluva long ago, I can tell you, refused under duress to cooperate with the government in a political scheme that would involve his company. One evening when the chap had just left his office to drive home, a black woman standing on the pavement suddenly stepped out in front of his car. The woman screamed in agony unable to move her leg. He told her to get into the back of his car and he would drive her to Barangwanath hospital, the hospital for blacks. Bystanders helped her in. He had not gone far when the police stopped him. They questioned the woman who said she was a prostitute and the driver had picked her up! Poor sucker, he was taken to the blerrie police station and charged under the Immorality Act. The woman walked off unharmed.

Next thing, his picture was on the front pages of all the papers with the details of his crime. His children were ridiculed at school and his wife, who did not believe a word of the scandal, was out of her mind. The chap was ostracised publicly and socially. He committed suicide soon afterwards. Can you imagine that people are scared not to cooperate? And, they always get you if you don't."

If my plea of "not guilty" could help the anti apartheid movement overseas to expose the evils of the system, as Max predicted it could, I would live each day of the trial with that purpose in mind. I felt suddenly that the whole process was worthwhile, that I had a personal mission and I looked forward to the challenge. My new resolve would help me to withstand the insults, ridicule and any other form of disparagement that might come my way. Well, that was what I hoped!

On the second evening of my visit, Boetie and I had a beer before dinner and sat watching the sunset on the horizon. I was pleased of the opportunity to have a quiet, private word with him,

"Things are particularly tough at the moment, Boetie, you know that. For some reason I cannot fathom, Alysha seems to feel insecure and doubts my love for her. This court case makes it worse because we cannot have any contact with each other at all. Granted, it was a difficult position to be in even before all this because we hardly ever saw each other. There is no other woman in my life and I am not interested in anyone else but when the picture of Barbara and me appeared in the paper for example, Alysha was upset. She wrote saying she was jealous while there was nothing to be jealous of. I had a nice evening and that was that."

"You'll find out soon enough that women are unpredictable, sometimes unreasonable. You can pass some simple remark and the next thing they are upset. No ruddy reason that you can think of. Still beats me at times. Have you told her you love her?"

"Of course, soon after I met her and since then too."

"Not enough. They want to hear it regularly as though you didn't mean it the first time or the last time."

"That's simple for rule number one."

"Ja, but the important part is that you have to keep it up." There was a short thoughtful silence.

"You left England and came to this country for her didn't you?"

"Yes, hoping to marry her."

"Let's sum it up: you've told her you love her, though not often enough, you came to this country for her, she knows you want to marry her and as a result of everything you've sacrificed for her, you are in a blerrie awful mess. If that's not enough proof of a man's love then I'm damned if I know what is. That's what I mean; women think differently. There is no logic to their emotions. Let me give you a few guidelines.

Maybe in the future, you will say something wrong, unintentionally of course, and you will not know what it is; haven't a clue. You scratch your head but you will never be able to guess because it could be something you said last week. In the meantime, she's been stewing over it. She did not like it then and she hates it now. This is where my advice comes in. *Never* ask her if it has anything to do with 'the time of the month!' However sympathetically you ask the question, she will blow her top. It seems to imply that her emotional state is dependent on her mood swings and could not possibly have anything to do with you."

"Thanks. I'll remember that."

"Another time you might ask her what's bugging her because you can see something is, and she will probably say 'Nothing' in a tone of voice that makes quite clear that you should know what it is - but you haven't a clue! Take her word for it and don't argue. Best leave it, go off and have a beer or something. If you try to find out what 'nothing' is, you make the situation worse. They have their idiosyncrasies, women, Annabel included, but I must admit I'm a lucky bugger. Annabel is a gem. No insults intended to women, but you know where you stand with okes."[2]

I chuckled as I often did at Boetie's colloquialisms.

"Believe me no woman will ever be a Minister of Finance not in this country nor in any other country. It has never happened in the past and it never will happen in the future. Why? Because they have their own bookkeeping system that only they collectively understand. For example, I received a helluva bill from the Posts and Telegraphs. I paid it and asked Annabel to look through it. She found a mistake. She had phoned her mother in England on her birthday and had a long chat. The account itemised three calls of equal length on the same day so I queried the account at the post office and received a refund. Clerical error, they said. I told Annabel. Next thing she goes shopping and comes home with a swimsuit "to die for" she tells me. Exclusive and sexy you could see that.

"Plan to take up swimming?" I ask. "Never seen her dip a toe in the pool."

"No, just need a new bathing costume" she answers, "I bought this with the money we made."

"Money we made?"

"Yes – the money we got back from the post office for those calls we didn't make!"

"You're not serious," I laughed.

"No kidding."

"Anything else I should be warned about?" I asked, enjoying his anecdotes.

---

2   Afrikaans slang for men

"Ja, there's shopping. Sooner or later, every husband has his own experience. I went once and never again. A gallery in Johannesburg had organised an exhibition of my paintings and the gallery owner wrote that he had organised a big bash with the Mayor of Johannesburg opening it and many VIPs with too much money and too little culture invited.

Annabel said she needed a special evening dress for the occasion and she wanted me to go with her to choose it. We travelled to Durban especially. She took me into what she called 'the best boutique in town', thick plush carpets, chandeliers, mirrors, the blerrie lot. You name it, they've got it. Two women, la-dada, hot potato in the mouth, you know the type, seated me in an exclusive room with two French brocade chairs, at least that is what Annabel said they were, gave me tea and said Madame (pronounced the French way if you please) would come through to model the outfits. Madame turned out to be Annabel. Annabel came through wearing a long, slinky, sexy white dress; a knock-out. I asked what it cost and nearly choked when I heard the amount. It nearly knocked *me* out.

'Madame is the image of Jackie Kennedy in that gown; every inch as elegant!' the women waxed lyrical while Annabel paraded before me like Jackie Kennedy herself. Sensing my lack of enthusiasm about the price, and I don't think that was too blerrie difficult, the women suggested that Madame try on the other gown.

"Oh yes, I'll do that for you, Boetie" says Annabel all excited. I note that it is no longer a dress but a gown!

I say no thanks to another cup of tea and wait.

One of the women helps Annabel change in a different room while the other one stays behind and says, 'Dressed in that *marvellous* white gown, Madame reminds me of Snow White, dark hair, beautiful fair skin, blue eyes.' I'm about to retort when Madame comes back looking like Mother Hubbard in a ruddy hideous dress! Swear to God, never seen such an eyesore. To begin with, I don't know whether it's supposed to be yellow or green. I immediately say no to this one and don't bother to tell me the price. 'You've got dresses a damn sight better than this at home,' I say to Snow White trying to get her feet back on the ground."

"You won't regret your choice, Sir, says one of the women. Madame looks gorgeous in the Dior creation". Now I note it is no longer a 'gown' but a 'creation!' "It arrived from Paris two days ago and there isn't another one like it."

"I came to the not particularly intelligent conclusion that the price tag determined whether it was a creation, a gown or simply an evening dress."

"Will you be paying cash or by cheque?" asks the more businesslike of the two.

That confounds me; I'm struck dumb for a moment because I don't know I've made a blerrie choice!

Annabel thanks me extravagantly and the next thing I know, we are on our way out of the best boutique in town, *me* carrying the ruddy box the size of a suitcase and what does it contain? Make no mistake; the slinky white Dior creation no less. Annabel is bucked, tells me I have fabulous taste and thanks me for choosing such a gorgeous creation, how generous I am! You can ruddy well say that again I think to myself but what could I say except tell her she looked a million dollars in it while I mull over the fact that there must have been a whole range of goddamn dresses between the Jackie Kennedy and the Mother Hubbard!

After that experience, I have never been conned into another shopping spree. They took me for a ruddy ride, all three of them; - *and how!*" he said with amusement." That was one Boetie's admirable features; he had been outmanoeuvred and he could see the funny side of it.

I felt better for having mentioned my concern to him. It seemed less serious somehow especially as we laughed at his shopping expedition, he remembering it and me picturing it.

Newly energised at the end of three days having benefited from Boetie and Annabel's hospitality, their understanding and their cheerful company and feeling better able to face being the centre of a potentially widely publicised court case, I decided to go back to Maritzburg.

Boetie stood at the side of the car to wave me off when Pauline came running towards us waving the morning paper. She was quite out of breath and excited. She handed the paper to Boetie saying,

"She's so pretty! Isn't she pretty, Daddy?"

"Ja, she sure is," Boetie answered as he studied the front page before handing the paper to me.

I was taken aback to see a large and very serene picture of Alysha that graced the front page under the bold headline, "Immorality Case, Woman's Identity revealed." A lengthy article followed. I could hardly take my eyes off the picture that portrayed not only the loveliness of Alysha's face but also her refinement.

Annabel came walking towards us; she had seen the picture and headlines. She and Boetie were intrigued not only by the serenity of the woman who looked back at them through calm, steadfast, almond-shaped eyes but also by her virtuous expression. They had heard so much about her in the last few days but had no idea what she looked like. Her face had been a mystery until that moment. I handed the newspaper back to Boetie saying I would read it later.

Alysha's photograph in the paper was sure to stir up even more public interest and that would go down well with the media but probably not with the State that wanted the circumstances and characters to be portrayed in the worst possible light.

On arrival, I drove straight to the Police Station to report my presence, as I was required to do on a daily basis. The officer at the desk told me that Detective Viljoen would be at the station in ten minutes and wanted to see me. Shortly afterwards, I was taken to a large, windowless room where the only furniture was a table and two chairs and a light bulb that dangled from the ceiling. The atmosphere was intimidating.

"Please take a seat Mr. Sinclair. I have a proposal to make that may help you out of the predicament in which you find yourself. It is like this. If you plead "guilty" to the charge against you, you will be able to leave the country without a sentence, not even a suspended sentence. The bail will be refunded. You are a foreigner in our land and I can assure you that the sort of publicity you will receive in a case of this nature, particularly as a visiting intellectual, will not be in your professional or personal interests. We both know that you are guilty, do we not Mr. Sinclair? A plea to this effect will save you the humiliation of going through a public trial."

"Mr. Viljoen, I have always believed that a suspect is innocent until proven guilty. Your assumption is that I am guilty without you even having questioned me. Innocence or guilt in a case like this is open to conjecture. I have no intention of pleading guilt."

"You have a few days to reconsider your standpoint Mr. Sinclair and I advise you most strongly to follow the most sensible course open to you. If you do not change your mind, then wheels will be set in motion for your trial. Good day, Mr. Sinclair."

I had a very strong feeling that Detective Viljoen wanted the easy way out not in my best interests but in his own.

I arrived back at the flat to find that Wisdom had completed re-filing my papers. As far as the incoming post was concerned, I noted wryly that there were piles of "hate mail" and a very small, pathetic pile of "friendly mail." I did not intend to read any of them. There were a few personal letters but those too could wait. The flat was neat and tidy and I presumed that Wisdom had gone to lunch. When he had not returned by dinnertime I became anxious and went in search of Mdala. I tracked him down and when I asked about Wisdom, he said,

"Sir, the police came today and took him away. I do not like it."

It was a relief when Wisdom came to work on time the next morning. He looked glum and exhausted. When I asked him where he had been, he said he could not talk.

"Sir, I had to swear on the life of Ugogo that I will not talk to you about the court case because I must be a witness." He was close to tears.

"Skivvy, I want you to pack your clothes and leave today for the kraal. The police have your details so they will know where to find you when they need you."

"I don't want to leave you, Sir," he said as he wiped his moist eyes on his sleeve.

"I appreciate that, Skivvy, but it is for the best. I will miss you but I'm not working so I can look after myself."

Charles and Ugogo would take care of Wisdom and he would be safe with them. I gave him a generous amount of money to tide him over for however long the nasty business of a court case would last.

I phoned Alysha that night and we spoke of ourselves, of how we felt and of our love for each other. The last time we had managed a personal conversation was on the plane from Delhi. I decided that I would phone her every night bearing in mind that our phones were being tapped.

I asked Alysha about Goofy and Mira and she said they had been so distressed by the events of that night that they had not gone on holiday to Mauritius the next day as planned. Her parents were distressed, very disappointed that she had pursued her relationship with me but they were bearing up well under the circumstances. Since her picture had appeared in the papers, Pitajee had received many kind messages from friends and from business people in all sections of the community and that had cheered him. Alysha said she could hardly keep up with the piles of letters she had received and continued to receive from staff members, students, past students and others who regarded the unpleasant publicity with compassion. I was reassured about the well-being of the Patel family and was grateful for that.

"How does the Indian community, well I suppose I mean more your friends, feel about your relationship with a white man?"

"They do not commit themselves to an opinion but they definitely think I have been incredibly stupid. Everyone who knows our family sympathises with Ma and Pitajee because I have not conformed to our cultural traditions. Indians believe that any Hindu who voluntarily chooses not to observe our customs is extremely foolish. Not one of them would want to be in my shoes and not in my parents' shoes either."

"I am so relieved that you are not being ostracised. I hate to think of the misery you must be enduring. If it's any comfort, Darling, remember I love you!"

"And I love you Roger – with all my heart."

Next, I phoned Max. He was happy about the publicity and the intense interest being generated in the case. He told me that the Court would contact him when a date had been set for the trial to begin and he would then get in touch with me immediately.

The last phone call I made was to my parents. They had not heard or read anything about the case so I was able to put them in the picture and to assure them that they should not worry. Dad said they would fly out to me immediately if I needed moral support but they would await further details. Naturally, they were concerned he said.

It had been a long day. Those close to me had given me encouragement and support but I had to face the music alone. I flopped into bed.

Twelve

As far as I could make out, the hype surrounding my arrest had died down. The subpoena I received arrived two weeks before the trial was to due begin and apart from a small, insignificant paragraph in the newspaper, there was no further mention of the court case.

Max's driver called for me at the flat on the first morning of the trial and drove me to the hotel where Max was staying. We had a cup of coffee together before driving to the Magistrate's Court in Pietermaritzburg. When we arrived, we were confronted with an amazing scene. There were hundreds of people gathered outside with tens of police officers in attendance. Many people were holding up banners only one of which I could read from the car, "Jail the Professor." I was pleased I could not read more of them!

"Surely these people are not all here for my trial?"

"There is no other case being heard today. They are all here for you, the antagonists and protagonists.

"I doubt whether there are many protagonists from what I see."

As we stepped out of the car in front of the building, the flashlights of dozens of cameras blinded us.

We paused on the steps of the building and I saw to my left that there was a gathering of men on Harley Davidson motorbikes. As if by some involuntary action, I lifted my arm to them and the sound of them revving their engines was deafening. A police guard hurried us indoors. I thought only of my Harley Davidson friends. We were a club of about twenty-five members so every member must have taken time off work to be there. It is odd that in such a nerve-wrecking situation, I concentrated my mind on such an inconsequential detail.

Max and I took our seats beside each other in a crowded, silent courtroom. We had our backs to the gallery so I could not see who was there and was pleased about that. The Judge and two Assessors entered the courtroom and everyone stood up. Then the official preliminaries took place and everyone sat down again.

The Prosecutor called the Witness No 1. Who might that be I wondered?

Mdala took to the witness stand! He was obviously nervous and kept his eyes cast down. He might have been an amusing figure in his incongruous outfit had there not been a touch of sadness about his appearance. He was wearing Wilson's black trousers that he had rolled up at the ankles because they were too long and the top buttons of the trousers had, of necessity, not been done up. The white shirt was a touch too tight around his waist and the sleeves hung half way down his hands. He wore shiny new black shoes!

Mdala answered all the questions put to him in a firm voice. He gave his Zulu name in full, stated his occupation,

"Flat boy for thirty five years in the same place. Boss boy and watchman for no extra charge." He swore to tell the truth, the whole truth and nothing but the truth. Then the cross-examination began.

"Have you ever seen women going into Mr. Sinclair's flat?"

"Yebo[3], only one."

"Was she a white woman or a black woman?"

"A white woman."

"Did you often see the white woman visiting the flat?"

"Yebo, I saw her every day, but she did not visit Sir Sinclair every day."

"Was that not strange?"

"Ikona[4]."

"Why is it not strange?"

Silence.

"Did you find out who the white woman was?"

"Yebo. She has been the supervisor of the flats for eleven years."

The Prosecutor raised his eyes to the ceiling, beseechingly.

"Did Mr. Sinclair ever give you money to keep quiet about the people who went to his flat?"

"That would be money for nothing. Sir Sinclair never gave money for nothing not even for information."

"Did you give Mr. Sinclair information?"

"Yebo."

"Can you tell the court what information you gave him?"

"I went to see Sir Sinclair one night to warn him about people who stood outside watching him at six o'clock every Sunday morning when Sir Sinclair went out. I told him that people, always the same people stood under the trees and they wrote down about him in their books. They kept writing. When I told Sir Sinclair, he did not like it but he was not worried. Even when he bought a motorbike, he still went out at six o'clock in the morning and for a long time the people stood writing notes. Sir Sinclair did not worry about my information and he did not pay me. I did not warn Sir Sinclair again. That was not because he did not pay me. I did not mind that he did not pay me but why warn someone who took no notice? I was worried."

---

3   Yes
4   No

"Why were you worried?"

"Because I did not trust people standing at my flats taking notes so early on Sunday morning."

"Did Sir … did *Mr.* Sinclair ever have a black woman or an Asian woman in his flat?"

"Ikona, I do not think he did. You see I always know what is going on and I never knew about that."

"Can you say for sure that no black woman and no Asian woman visited Mr. Sinclair in his flat?"

"I cannot say that. I can only say that I never saw such a thing. Even the people taking notes at six o'clock in the morning were all white people and not black people."

"That will be all thank you." Mdala left the dock without looking to his left or to his right. .

The Clerk of the Court called out, "Witness Number 2."

Witness Number 2 was Wisdom. I was appalled when I saw him. His face was grotesquely swollen. He was wearing Mdala's flat boys uniform with the long pants. The trousers were too short as were the sleeves of his shirt. The shirt and trousers were too wide around his middle and were bunched into a belt. He wore takkies. His dress code puzzled me because he always took pride in looking good. When asked his name, Wisdom seemed to have difficulty in answering.

"Andile Nklakanyno Mabena."

"Occupation?"

"Right Hand Man." The Prosecutor did not question Wisdom's unique title nor did he ask what a Right Hand Man's duties entailed.

Wisdom then requested a translator as he wished to give his evidence in Zulu.

I leaned over and told Max that I believed Wisdom was in trouble, certainly in pain if not mentally disturbed.

Max stood up, "My client requests that before the proceedings continue, Witness Number 2 be given medical attention."

The judge asked Wisdom if he was unfit to continue and he nodded. He was given permission to leave the stand. The court recessed while the witness was examined by a physician.

Forty minutes later, the court proceedings continued without Wisdom.

"Witness Number 3." Witness number three, was one of the police officers who had arrested me. Questions and answers were straightforward and boring; at least in my opinion. Perhaps others listened with avid interest. Everything was repeated and recorded exactly as it had happened.

"Witness Number 4" was the officer who had been present to assist with my arrest. His testimony was equally long and tedious.

The judge adjourned the proceedings until 10.30 the following morning.

There was little for Max and me to discuss since no surprising evidence against me had been mentioned. We left the courthouse together to face another barrage of cameras. Questions were thrown at us from all sides. The crowds had not diminished.

I could not wait to get away from it all and was pleased to walk into the peace and quiet of my flat. Wisdom was not there so I phoned Max and asked him if he could find out what had happened to him. After much difficulty and hours of telephoning and being passed from one department to another, Max eventually discovered that Wisdom had been admitted to hospital with a dislocated jaw and concussion. How had that happened? No further details were available.

That evening Jeremy phoned and asked me if I would like him to pop round as he guessed I would be alone. I welcomed the idea and asked him to bring a copy of the evening paper.

Jeremy gave me the paper and the front page carried three pictures. The main one was of me with my arm up in recognition of the Harley Davidson club, my only obvious supporters. There were pictures of people carrying apartheid placards, those who wanted to see the professor swing, and then a picture of a large group of Indian academics who had travelled many miles only to be refused entry to the courtroom.

There was a sarcastic article on the ill-informed and unexpected international reaction to the case. Outside interference was not appreciated. The article mentioned that an anti-apartheid movement in London planned a demonstration outside South Africa House that weekend to draw attention to the iniquities of the South African apartheid laws. For me that was a positive step since exposing the system was, I had to remind myself, my mission.

Jeremy asked me how I was feeling and then he managed to skirt around the proceedings of the day. How he did that was a miracle of mental and verbal agility. He must have had a natural talent or his skill was thanks to his political manoeuvrings. I appreciated his gesture in coming but the atmosphere was loaded with the weight of the unmentioned issue of the court case. His determination to avoid what was uppermost in our minds was surprising after the supportive letter he had written. Not feeling in the mood for such superficiality, I finally suggested that it might be a good idea if I had an early night. Jeremy was relieved I could see that. He had demonstrated his friendship, wished me all the luck in the world and was able to leave without having entered into a discussion of any relevance. I sent my regards to Sally.

I poured myself a Scotch and picked up the South African book I was reading "Valley of the Vines" by Joy Packer and puzzled over Jeremy's visit. It dawned on me that Jeremy was scared of rocking his political boat. He had had second thoughts since writing that letter to me. His aspirations for a leading position in the United Party did not allow him to say anything that might reek of collusion with me. He could not afford partisanship. I had after all contravened one of the most sacred of all South Africa's laws, the Immorality Act. I wondered if he was successful in his quest for a leadership position, whether Jeremy would have the backbone required for the job. If he campaigned, he would need courage. In northern Natal, not much more than a hundred miles from Pietermarizburg, Afrikaans-speaking Nationalist supporters wielding bicycle chains regularly broke up United Party meetings. Opposition leaders speaking in those areas, required physical as well as moral courage and police protection that was sadly lacking. The police, normally tough and quick to act, seemed immobilized or unprepared to deal with the violence at those meetings. The media called the meetings robust but that was in fact a euphemism for the thuggery that took place.

The United Party was the only major opposition party to the ruling government and was the party to which English-speaking citizens belonged and for which they voted. Their platform was the scrapping of "petty apartheid" but the ideology of grand apartheid remained intact.

The Progressive Party that proposed to scrap apartheid if elected was small and insignificant in terms of numbers and its leader Mrs. Helen Suzman, was a lonely voice in parliament. I reflected on the political scene and realised how involved I was with life in South Africa – metaphorically and literally!

The crowds outside the court were even greater the next day and I was self-conscious of my every movement knowing that people were observing me from all angles and the cameras continued to flash non-stop.

For no apparent reason, at least none that Max and I were aware of, the Judge postponed the hearing until five days later and that happened to be the following Monday.

Boetie phoned and suggested that I spend the days with them but I decided to go climbing in the mountains. Max confirmed with the Judge that this would be in order and I breathed a sigh of relief that I could escape temporarily from the crazy circus of media and public attention.

The international press association had sent representatives to report on the trial and they added to the pandemonium outside the Court. Many of them had permission to be inside the

Courtroom where, thankfully, no photography was permissible. It was difficult to keep my "crime" in perspective and I was inclined to lose sight of what it was! The hearing had lasted for only two days, though the trial had started a week previously, and already I had discovered that the euphoria of my mission deserted me as soon as I was alone.

The joy and uninterrupted happiness of our days in Jaipur might never have existed for all the contact I had with Alysha or anyone else important to me. Alysha had had to leave her home in Reservoir Hills for an unknown destination because the media was hounding her. Indian photographers, both local and overseas, camped outside the gates hoping to catch a glimpse of her. They described her as the most beautiful mistress of the century, a dubious compliment for someone as dignified and modest as Alysha.

The hotel staff welcomed me in their usual friendly manner and behaved as though they had never heard of a court case, let alone mine. The Indian waiters' attitude was particularly solicitous so I knew they were not only aware of the headline news but they were also sympathetic.

I climbed the superb mountains from sunrise to sunset every day. At the end of four days, I was refreshed in body and mind and was as ready as I would ever be to face a continuation of the trial for which I felt personally ill equipped. I had never been one to seek attention and had always stood in the shadow of my more extrovert brothers. On the other hand, perhaps no individual could feel prepared for the ordeal of facing an antagonistic world of self-righteous human beings who had no sympathy for, or understanding of those who walked outside the straight and narrow confines of their "moral" society.

I went back to Maritzburg and to the trial that began the following morning.

Witness Number 2 was called to the dock. I was most relieved to see Wisdom looking well. His swollen face was back to normal proportions. He still wore Mdala's uniform, for whatever reason he had for doing so. This time he did not ask for a translator.

In answer to the standard questions, he gave his name, "Andile Nklakanyno Mabena" and then he promised to tell the truth, the whole truth and nothing but the truth as had the previous witnesses.

"Did Mr. Sinclair entertain women in his flat?"

"Not during the day. My job ended at around 5 o'clock, sometimes later, so I do not know who Sir Sinclair entertained in his flat at night."

"Did you ever see signs in the morning that a woman had been there the night before?"

There was a long silence.

"Will the witness please answer the question?"

There was another long silence.

"The witness is required to answer the question."

I wondered why Wisdom was not answering the question. Then finally, he did.

"I'm trying to think what signs I should have seen if there was a woman in Sir Sinclair's flat."

"Was there lipstick on a cup, for example?" The Prosecutor asked in desperation. Wisdom took his time thinking about it.

"That would be a white woman," he said finally as though still thinking about the question.

"Nooo," he said slowly and looked at the Prosecutor expectantly waiting for the next clue.

"Did you smell perfume in the flat?"

There was silence. Wisdom narrowed his eyes deep in thought and then he repeated,

"Perfume?" Once again, he waited expectantly.

There was twittering amongst the spectators.

"Did you ever see women's lingerie in the flat?"

"No, I never saw women lingering in the flat."

A wave of suppressed laughter filled the courtroom.

"Did you see items of women's underwear in the flat?"

He held his chin obviously trying to recall such an item.

"Nooo. Never saw under clothing, never saw over clothing." His expressions were priceless and the spectators burst out laughing.

The Clerk of the Court called for "Silence in Court!"

The Prosecutor changed his line of questioning,

"Did Mr. Sinclair ever pay you to keep quiet about the women he entertained?"

"Sir Sinclair has never asked me, or paid me, to be quiet about anything and he has never asked me to be dishonest."

"Did you ever see an Asian woman in Mr. Sinclair's flat?"

"Asian?"

"Indian."

"I never saw an Asian Indian woman, never saw a white woman, only Mrs. van Niekerk, never saw a Coloured woman, never saw a black woman in Sir Sinclair's flat."

There was more sniggering.

"The Witness is required to answer only the question put to him!"

"Do you know where Sir … *Mr.* Sinclair went at 6 o'clock on Sunday mornings?"

"I did not work on Sundays. I would not have asked him. That was not my business."

"So you do not know where Mr. Sinclair went so early on Sunday mornings?"

"No."

The judge interrupted the exchange to ask whether there was any purpose to the cross examination unless the Prosecutor was attempting to expose a fact not yet clear to the bench."

"No further questions," the Prosecutor said irritably.

Max leaned over and remarked to me, "He expected to exhort incriminating evidence from his Number 1 and Number 2 witnesses. The Prosecution does not believe that you never entertained Miss Patel in your flat."

Listening to Wisdom give his evidence, I was much impressed that his command of the English language and his pronunciation were excellent. He had done his best to learn and he had mimicked my manner of speech.

The next person to be called to the dock was Detective Viljoen.

I had expected that the prosecutor would call Mrs. van Niekerk to the witness stand but she had probably been interrogated beforehand and would have had no more important information to impart than that she had suspected all along that I was a Commie. She would say that I had lied to her about that and she could kick herself for believing me! Mrs. van Niekerk had not appeared at my flat since the news broke in the papers, not even to say, "Well, I told you so."

In answer to a question from the Prosecutor, Detective Viljoen told the Court that there was indisputable evidence that Miss Patel and Mr. Sinclair had been on holiday together in England the year before and they had been to India together only three weeks previously.

He was asked to tell the Court where his officers had arrested Mr. Sinclair.

"Two officers arrested Mr. Sinclair at the home of Dr. Godfrey *Govender* in Reservoir Hills." He emphasised the name probably to make sure that Govender, being an Asian name, was not lost on the Judge and Assessors.

The Prosecutor looked smug as though he had at last struck gold.

Detective Viljoen gave evidence seemingly to the satisfaction of the Prosecution because the Prosecutor smiled approvingly.

Max then stood up to cross-examine the police officer who had arrested me.

"Can you tell the Court the circumstances of the arrest?"

"We were informed by Detective Viljoen that Mr. Sinclair and Miss Patel had contravened the terms of the Immorality Act. On their return from a holiday together, we were further informed that Mr. Sinclair had been seen stepping into Mr. Govender's car at Louis Botha Airport. Miss Patel was already in the car. My instructions were to arrest Mr. Sinclair."

"Did Mr. Sinclair offer any resistance when you arrested him in Mr. Govender's home?"

"No. He was startled but not aggressive."

"At what time did you arrest Mr. Sinclair?"

"At exactly 3.42 a.m."

"Is that considered a civilized hour at which to make an arrest?"

"I carry out instructions."

"Was Mr. Sinclair in bed when you arrested him?"

"No, Mr. Sinclair was standing with Mr. Govender in the passageway of the house."

"So you did not see Mr. Sinclair in the same bedroom or in the same bed as Miss Patel?"

"No, but it was not my responsibility to see who was sleeping where or with whom. My task is to carry out orders and not to question them. My order was to arrest Mr. Sinclair and that is what I did."

Max then called Detective Viljoen, the detective assigned to the case, to take the stand.

"Detective Viljoen, did you give the order for Mr. Sinclair to be arrested."

"Yes, I did."

"Will you please tell the Court why you had Mr. Sinclair arrested?"

"The Accused, in full knowledge of the laws governing this country, contravened one of the cornerstones of our society, the Immorality Act. I therefore had him arrested."

"Did you have proof of his criminal intent?"

"Proof enough to bring him to trial. In my opinion, it was not intent, it was a fact."

"Will you clarify for this Court, your interpretation of the fact."

"The result of my department's investigation, was that Mr. Sinclair and Miss Patel, both of different racial groups, had a sexual relationship in contravention of the laws of this country."

"Please tell the Court how it was that you knew that Miss Patel and Mr. Sinclair had a sexual relationship."

"On two occasions they went on holiday together overseas."

"Did either Miss Patel or Mr. Sinclair or any other reliable source inform you that they had a sexual relationship while on holiday together?"

"No."

"Did they stay in the same hotel while away?"

"I believe so."

"Can you please tell the Court in which hotel they stayed."

"I cannot do that without recourse to Internal Security."

"Is it illegal for a couple belonging to different races to go overseas on holiday together?"

"It is not acceptable under South African law."

"Do you assume that those who go on holiday together sleep together?"

"Yes," the police officer put his finger around the inside of his collar as though to loosen it. "I can only judge the circumstances in this particular case."

"Judging by the circumstances in this particular case, do you know without a shadow of doubt that Miss Patel and Mr. Sinclair had a sexual relationship?"

"No. The object of this case is to establish the truth."

"It is indeed."

"Was it your duty as Detective in charge of this case, to recommend that Mr. Sinclair be arrested for the crime of sexual misconduct?"

"Yes. I believe all the circumstantial evidence points to Mr. Sinclair being guilty of sexual misconduct in terms of the Immorality Act."

"Do you suspect, or have any so-called circumstantial evidence, that Mr. Sinclair and Miss Patel broke the law while in South Africa."

"Yes, he was arrested in Mr. Govender's house and Miss Patel was present."

"When a man and a woman sleep in the same house, does that prove in your professional opinion that they sleep together? Bear in mind that they were not alone in the house."

"This is for the Court to decide."

"No more questions my lord."

The Prosecutor said that he would not be calling any further witnesses. Max confirmed that he would not cross-examine any further witnesses.

The Clerk of the Court called the Accused to the dock.

I swore to tell the truth, the whole truth and nothing but the truth.

"State name, nationality and profession."

"Roger Sinclair, British subject. Professor of Physics, PhD Oxford University. Present employment: Two-year contract with the Government of South Africa. Senior visiting lecturer at Witwatersrand University, University of Pretoria, Rand Afrikaans University, University of Natal, Stellenbosch University and University of Potchefstroom.

"Do you plead "guilty" or "not guilty" to the charges against you?

"Not guilty."

"Do you wish to say anything in your own defence before the bench considers its verdict?"

"Yes, I do. I am in full agreement with the evidence of all the witnesses. Their testimonies have been a fair reflection of the events as I experienced them. Regarding the question of innocence or guilt, I have to confess to the following:

I am guilty of loving Miss Alysha Patel.

I am guilty of wanting to marry her and to share the rest of my life with her. Of this, I am not ashamed.

I am guilty of having the highest respect for Miss Patel's exemplary moral standards and for her remarkable intelligence.

I am guilty of admiring Miss Patel's parents for their compassion, their strong family unity and love. Through this trial now taking place, I am guilty of causing them sadness and humiliation.

On all these accounts, I am guilty.

I am not guilty of causing harm or embarrassment to anyone other than the Patel family since my contacts with Miss Patel have always been private and discreet.

Under no circumstances am I guilty nor is Miss Patel guilty of immoral behaviour.

We conducted our love affair far beyond the borders of South Africa and we have not contravened the Immorality Act as it applies to life within this country.

I have nothing more to say."

The Court rested its case and adjourned for three days for the Judge and his two assessors to consider their verdict. Unless their verdict was to be "not guilty as charged," their decision would come as no surprise to anyone.

I was relieved that the trial had progressed as quickly as it had and that no one had attacked Alysha and me in an undignified or intimately insulting manner.

Max assured me that we would not get away with a "not guilty" verdict but the details of the case had been widely publicised overseas and consequently a further nail had been driven in the coffin of Apartheid. The demonstrations that had gone off peacefully in London, had received tremendous publicity and tens of thousands of people awaited the verdict with increasing interest. The story of two handsome, intelligent physicists who had fallen in love and had been harassed and victimised because of their colour had appealed to the romantic sentiments of the public in a way that no other had. Our photographs had been widely published.

That evening when once again experiencing the anti-climax that followed a day of intense concentration, the crowds and cameras, there was a knock at my front door. I opened it and was taken aback to see Charles Mkhize. He was wearing a flat-boy's uniform, with long trousers also trimmed in red!

"Good evening, Charles. This is a pleasant surprise. Come in."

"Good evening, Roger. I'm wearing this uniform for anonymity."

"Please sit down. Will you have a bite with me? Nothing special I'm afraid as I've had little time for grocery shopping and I've lost my appetite along the way."

Over a sandwich and a beer, Charles told me that Wisdom was leaving the country, had probably already left! I was stunned, lost for words.

How could you, Skivvy, without a word to me? How could you?

"The black population is following your case closely and we know that Wisdom is in for trouble when all this ends. The police picked him up the day before your trial began, took him to Head Quarters and interrogated him. When he insisted that he had not seen an Indian woman visit you in your flat, they physically abused him and the interrogation started again. As you know, he was badly beaten up. We are grateful that you intervened when he took the stand as a witness.

He was supposed to say that he had seen an Indian woman in your flat because that is what the police believe. The fact that he stuck to his word, spoke firmly and unflinchingly in the dock, will not stand him in good stead. In fact, none of the witnesses proved to be of any value to the prosecution and that must have been a body blow to the investigating detectives. They were convinced that when Mdala and Wisdom stood in the dock in that frightening, overwhelming situation, they would come up with evidence against you."

"I feel sorrier for those two men that I do for myself. Neither of them deserved this."

"No they didn't but they are heroes in their own communities. Mdala feels very important and revels in his celebrity. The Anti Apartheid Movement is impressed with Wisdom's bearing, his intelligence and his command of English. He now speaks with a British accent thanks to you! Political friends helped him this evening and to my knowledge, they have arranged for his escape to take place through the bush. We think, and hope, that he will soon be safely out of the country and that he will be able to join and assist important people working in Central African countries for the freedom of South Africa."

"I'm pleased too that he will soon be out of all this, Charles. I hope the plan will work and that he will not come to harm. I feel sad that I have not had the opportunity to say good-bye to him. His flight to an independent black country will provide him with the opportunity to fulfil his need to do something constructive in working towards a free and democratic South Africa. He, like millions of others, dreams of, and longs for the end of apartheid." I had a lump in my throat and could not speak for some minutes.

"How will Ugogo manage without financial help from Wisdom?'

"We look after each other as best we can."

"Will it be possible for me to send a contribution every month to make her life easier and in that way help Wisdom too?"

"You will not be able to get money to her from England or anywhere else outside the country so I suggest that you deposit however much you have in mind, in a Post Office account. I will arrange that for you if you so wish. We have a small post office about ten miles from the kraal."

"I have no idea how long I will be here after the verdict is handed down because of course I expect to be deported so the sooner you can organise this, the better."

We shook hands in the uniquely African manner. I did not know whether I would ever see Charles again but one way or another he would contact me regarding the best way of getting money to the post office nearest to the kraal. About an hour after he left, my doorbell rang again. I was in two minds about whether to open the door or not. I was beginning to feel edgy and did not feel like being sociable. The news of Wisdom troubled me and I was sad that I had not had a chance to speak to him since the awful drama began. I wanted to compliment him on his testimony, his courage and thank him for being one of the most honest, loyal and special people I had ever had the honour to call my friend.

Whoever it was at the door rang the bell with some persistence so I walked towards it. Slowly I opened the door and there was Barbara. Her face was tear-stained and her mascara was a bit smudgy from wiping her eyes I supposed.

"Barbara, what on earth are you doing here and what is the matter?" She flung herself into my arms and started crying.

I took her through to the sitting room and as I did so, the phone rang. It was my father.

"Roger, you and Alysha have been in our papers every day. The reports are scathing of Apartheid of course and therefore supportive of you. I guess it must be a vastly different story over there. Mum and I wonder whether you would like us to fly over to be with you when the verdict is handed down. It must be a traumatic time for you,"

"Thank you for your concern, Dad, but I know already that the verdict will go against me so I am prepared for the worst. I have had dozens of sympathy letters from around the world but I can count on one hand such letters from the white community here. This is something they don't understand. There have been a few supportive letters from local Indians but that is due no doubt to the fact that Alysha's father is prominent in the Indian community. I no longer open local mail unless I can see who the sender is. You will probably be seeing me soon so please don't waste your money on flying over."

"Will you come straight home?"

"Yes. Max expects me to be deported and the only question is how long I will have to pack up here. I have made a good start but I will miss my Right Hand Man when it comes to packing my books and academic materials. The Harley Davidson dealer bought back my motorbike at a good price so that was fortunate."

"O.K. Son, you sound pretty much in control so we'll await further news. Mum would like to speak to you."

Mum could not speak through her sniffling and apologised for having a beastly cold so I gave her my love and we rang off.

I went back to Barbara who was also sniffling, at least she was no longer crying.

"Come now Barbara, tell me all about it!"

"I'm sorry I'm being so silly. I would not have come had I know this was going to happen. Crying I mean. I think the emotion of the court case has got to me. You see I have been there every day and have lived through it. I admire you enormously for the way you coped through those difficult weeks. I even felt jealous and wished you had been speaking of me when you took the stand and spoke of Miss Patel! You looked so strong and confident, not at all cowered as the Prosecution had hoped and expected you would be. You are not only a strong man as far as character is concerned but you have a sensitive side too. I waited a long time to meet a man like you, and then when it happened, you loved someone else." She blew her nose again.

"Your words embarrass me Barbara but thank you for the best compliment I have ever had. Has there been much discussion of the case on campus?" I asked to divert her from her own misery.

"It's been riveting! There are divided opinions of course. A large section, particularly the men, said that you broke the law and should be punished accordingly. When they saw the pictures of Miss Patel in papers and magazines, they became noticeably less opinionated! The women have always admired you and now they think "what a waste!" As you know, we have a group of very vocal left-wing radicals amongst both lecturers and students. They have taken full advantage of the circumstances of this case. They have exploited to the hilt the fact that it is a case of love between intellectuals. This aspect has given them a terrific opportunity to expose the fanaticism and the vindictiveness of our Internal Security in upholding so-called public morality. The group is calling for the abolition not only of the Immorality Act but also of Apartheid but that is nothing new, they do it continually. I cannot see them getting away with their anti-apartheid rhetoric this time and feel sure that many of them will be arrested as Communist agitators. That does not bother them since they seem to be daring the authorities to detain them knowing that at this sensitive time of world attention, much publicity will be given to their arrests. So you see you have set the cat amongst the pigeons!"

Her long, uninterrupted monologue seemed to make Barbara feel better and I thought how unfortunate it was that we could not turn love on and off at will. How much simpler life would have been for me had I not been so much in love with Alysha that I could not feel a stirring in my heart for any other woman.

"In no time at all everyone will have forgotten the case." I responded. "The liberal students will leave university to get jobs and their responsibilities will be more important than any political views they may have held while students. The professors have their positions to consider and being government employees they cannot afford to raise their voices too loudly in opposition so I don't think the government takes their dissent very seriously. I doubt whether the government would play into the hands of the students by arresting anyone."

"You may be right. It shows how ineffectual we are to influence the government in any way."

"I haven't offered you anything to drink, can I do so now?"

"No, I'll be going now and I do feel better."

"I'm pleased about that. Thank you for your support Barbara. Had I not already been in love with Alysha, who knows what might have happened between you and me?" It was an unlikely scenario because if I had not loved Alysha, I would not have gone to South Africa in the first place.

Barbara was obviously delighted to hear that. Somehow, it helped to salvage her sense of pride, I guess; that of loving someone who did not return her love. I kissed her on both cheeks before I showed her to the door.

What an evening it had been!

Thirteen

The Courtroom was packed, both inside and out, for the verdict in the case of The State versus Roger Sinclair.

I was calm having no illusions as to the outcome. Max insisted that his fee had been taken care of and I could only guess by whom.

There was a short summary of the charges against me and then the Judge delivered his verdict from the bench. I was well aware of what he was saying but could not remember his exact words.

"The Accused has shown himself to be an intelligent person who having resided in South Africa for almost two years is well aware of our laws. According to the testimony of the Accused, he and Miss Patel conducted their love affair outside the borders of South Africa. Whether Mr. Sinclair and Miss Patel conducted their affair only outside the borders of South Africa is a matter for speculation. The Accused has not proved to the satisfaction of this Court that he has not contravened the terms of the Immorality Act and I therefore find him Guilty!"

To expect a guilty verdict and to hear it announced, were two different things. I felt deeply wounded. I had been tried, judged and found to be a criminal.

As soon as the judge had announced his verdict, a deafening noise from the crowds gathered outside resounded through the Courtroom. I guessed it was cheering. There was dead silence inside.

The verdict had been arrived at. Now for the sentence:

"The Accused is sentenced to two years imprisonment suspended for two years on condition that he does not contravene the terms of the Immorality Act during that time. A fine of Seven Thousand Rand is imposed and the Accused must leave South Africa within the period of one month from to-day's date."

More prolonged cheering from outside. Was it jeering? Perhaps the masses considered the sentence too lenient. I would not have been shocked at any reaction from that crowd. Still, the thought of facing those hardliners was a daunting prospect. I knew then that it was not possible for the average person to be psychologically prepared for an experience of this nature. I certainly was not. Max had warned me before the case started that it would require courage, stamina and a strong heart! I hoped I had those qualities that had not been fully tested until that moment.

Max and I took leave of each other outside, perhaps never to meet again. We shook hands and he said,

"Good luck Roger, you did well." With that, he walked over to his car.

Did well? I had been found guilty, given a hefty fine, a suspended prison sentence and a deportation charge. I had lost my reputation, at least locally, some friends, I had a criminal record and all my lawyer could say was that I had done well!

Max had carried out his job professionally. For him, it was simply that, a job, and one that he hoped would benefit his own cause.

The feeling of abandonment, of isolation was crushing in the face of the vitriolic crowd that waited patiently to catch a close-up glimpse of me in my car, me the despised "sexual offender." The cameras clicked and flashed; pictorial evidence of a condemned man.

When I arrived at my flat building, an uplifting sight confronted me; riders, my friends, on their Harley Davidson machines. As I stepped out of the car, the riders revved up their engines and as one, they all raised an arm in greeting; a solid blur of hands. I acknowledged their salute and about two minutes later, they rode away leaving behind a deathly silence. Bemused, I walked upstairs to my second-floor flat and to my astonishment saw Boetie at my front door.

"No ruddy excuses, my friend, you are coming home with me. You have a whole month to prepare for your departure. Annabel has your room ready, Samuel has prepared your favourite babotie for dinner and the girls cannot wait to see you again and give you all the sympathy in the world. Take your time to pack your bag. I shall sit in the lounge and wait for you.

Boetie managed to make dramatic circumstances seem so normal. He, the Afrikaner Boetie, and the black man, Wisdom, were two people I would never forget, not if I lived to be a hundred years old.

Before I had completed the little packing I had to do, the phone rang. It was Alysha's father, Mr. Patel,

"Roger, I'm so pleased this whole nasty case is over. How are you feeling?"

"Pretty shattered really. I expected the verdict and yet to hear myself convicted of a criminal offence was soul-destroying."

"I can imagine. Chin up! I want you to know that Alysha sends her love. She is still at a secret address and plans to stay there until the public and media have lost interest in her. That should not take long now that the case is over. She will contact you in due course. In the meantime, my wife joins me in congratulating you on the manner in which you have endured the publicity, the proceedings and we thank you for the kind words you spoke about us. We appreciate that. You did well and our Indian community have nothing but praise for you. Goofy and Mira have lived through this whole experience with you, or at least they think they have. Goofy went to Maritzburg but the officials denied him entry to the courtroom. No Asians were allowed in. The Govenders are playing it low key until publicity has died down. Anyway, we shall keep in touch. Look after yourself."

"Namaste Mr. Patel and thanks for calling. Please tell Alysha that I love her and long to see her again." I wondered where Alysha was staying, where was her secret address? Anyhow, her father sounded comfortable with it so he must have felt satisfied about her security. You could never tell in this country because when it came to race relations, there were plenty of fanatics around.

I spent four peaceful days with Boetie and Annabel. Just as on the previous occasion, I was able to recharge my batteries to face the world of racial discrimination and hatred.

The three girls tried to cheer me up, no doubt thinking I needed it, to the extent that Annabel had to rescue me from their non-stop attention. They dragged me into the swimming pool, onto the tennis court, into games of scrabble and worst of all, "Guess what?"

The youngest of the girls, Pauline, asked me confidentially, "Uncle Roger, do you really love an *Indian*?"

"Yes, I do. Do you think that is strange, Pauline?"

"I don't know, I have never heard of anyone loving an Indian before."

"I believe that all people are equal, whatever their colour, and we should get to know them before judging them. Don't you think so?"

"Yes, I do and that's what Mummy says too." That was the only reference any of the girls made to the Court case.

When I arrived back at my flat, I knew that I had managed to get the excruciating experience into perspective. I could afford seven thousand rand, I was not going to jail and I was richer for the South African experience, the good and the bad. On balance, I had to be pleased.

I had only just sat down when Mrs. van Niekerk came to the door. She was highly upset. I invited her in.

"Mrs. van Niekerk, is something wrong?"

"Ja, you can say that again because I feel bad. I feel *so* bad. It's all my fault," she answered in a shaky voice.

"Come now. What's all your fault?"

"I listened to all that skinnering about you and all those complaints. I shouldn't have stopped you taking the natives for rides on your motorbike. I didn't know how lonely you were. I didn't know that you would turn to an Indian woman for company. How could I know that?" Mrs. van Niekerk wiped her eyes. "If I'd known you were lonely I would've introduced you to Sannie's daughters. That's what I would've done. Ilona has a very good job; she's a shorthand typist for Macey's Motor Repairs. They think very highly of her. Now that says something. Elsa is even prettier than Ilona and she's a cashier at Tasty Bite's Drive-In restaurant. She's the queen-pin there. Lovely girls if I say so myself. I would've introduced you."

"Mrs. van Niekerk, whatever trouble I have 'landed up in' is entirely of my own doing. You did your best to advise me but I was already in love with Miss Patel. You couldn't help that and I couldn't help that either. I am sure that your nieces are charming girls but meeting them would not have helped in my situation but thank you anyway."

"They are not my nieces but I wish they were because I haven't got any. Well, it's too late now more's the shame. It's no good crying over spilt milk. When Mdala reported to me that the police had barged into your flat I came straight here and when I saw them throwing your things out of the drawers, I ordered them to stop.

'Don't you dare touch Mr. Sinclair's things, he's not a commie and he's not a kaffir-boetie!

One of the policemen said,

'Did we say he was?'

'I'm not saying what you said I'm telling you what I know.' I told him straight but they took no notice of me and I couldn't stop them from throwing everything out of your drawers.

'I am the Supervisor of these flats so I would know if Mr. Sinclair is a commie or a kaffir-boetie – and he is not! Show some respect for my job when I tell you something,' I told them. They didn't, they turned on me instead.

'Did you see an Indian woman in this flat?' the bigger policemen shouted at me as though I had done something wrong even if I had seen her.

'Are you *batty*?' I asked him. 'And there's no need to shout!' I told him as plainly as I am telling you now. 'No Indians come here. Mdala knows everyone who comes and goes. He reports any funny goings-on to me and he has never reported this.' They didn't like that - not one bit I can tell you. Do you think I could care? No, I couldn't care less about those two domkops. They asked me again about the Indian woman as though I was on trial for seeing somebody.

'I've told you I have never seen an Indian woman around here. I must say it's *so nice* to have planks for policemen!' I told them. Well I can tell you they didn't like that either but they couldn't arrest me for calling them planks. You can't arrest people for things like that. Then they said they would get me in court and that I would have to tell the truth about the Indian woman.

'Please yourselves.' I said, 'If I haven't seen an Indian woman, then I haven't seen an Indian woman and I won't say I've seen what I haven't seen.' That put them in their place.

'You might as well know' I said, 'that I will not say *anything* against Mr. Sinclair that isn't true not in court and not out of court either.' I told them that without blinking an eye. 'If you make me testify' I told them, 'I will tell the truth and say that Mr. Sinclair is the best rooinek I ever met even if he has slept with an Indian woman that I didn't know about.' And that's the truth."

"I'm proud of you for being so brave, Mrs. van Niekerk. Not many people would dare to speak to policemen like that. Have you found in life that if we do what we believe to be right, things usually turn out for the best in the end? However bad it seems now, I'm convinced that this situation too will turn out for the best."

"No, I've never thought like that." She paused obviously considering a new angle.

"Ja, you're right," she said slowly. "When I think of that double-crossing big-bellied bastard Stoffel van Niekerk ..." her voice trailed off. "His family blamed me for not having children and then none of his wives had children. That turned out right for me in the end!" Tears spilled over and I knew they were not for me.

"Mrs. van Niekerk, you're a friend. When I am back in my own cold, rainy place, I will think of how beautifully you furnished this flat." She smiled through her tears.

Women in tears were a new experience for me and one I hoped would not be repeated ever if that were possible. Impulsively, I put my arm around her slender shoulders. I felt a stab of pity for the vulnerable, well-meaning woman who had not an ounce of malice in her. She had her own interests to consider yet found herself at an emotional crossroads with tears in her eyes. Mrs. van Niekerk was no different from the average South African who lived an insular existence; she was not responsible for her intrinsic fears and prejudices. She, a victim of years of brainwashing, saw life through her own narrow experience and she tried valiantly to protect her own interests. Mrs. van Niekerk understood loneliness as only a lonely person could and she forgave me everything because of what she perceived to be my loneliness.

I said I would call in to say goodbye before I left. "So your advice was almost spot-on Mrs. van Niekerk; I have been deported but they asked a lot of questions first and they didn't bundle me onto the first plane so I'm lucky after all!"

"Ag shame, I wish I was wrong," she said and then added that she couldn't talk anymore. I offered her a drink and she said she wouldn't be able to swallow it.

Mdala had seen me arriving back and he came to my door as soon as Mrs. van Niekerk left,

"Sir," he said, "the flat boys and I want to know if you need any help. Wisdom has gone. I read a little English but the younger ones are better so you can choose."

"Thank you very much Mdala. I think your English is more than good enough. I would appreciate your help."

Mdala's grin became an involuntary chuckle.

"I can come to your flat at four o'clock every afternoon."

"Excellent, can you start tomorrow afternoon?"

"Thank you, Sir."

With Mdala's help, the packing of all my books was accomplished in a couple of days. "International Removals" arrived and when the boxes had all been taken away, the flat was devoid of my personal possessions. It felt empty and soulless. I could not bear to stay there.

The work done, I asked Mdala if he would like to have dinner with me,

"Shall I get a take-away?"

I could not have done Mdala a greater favour. He was jubilant. I realised he had envied, if not resented, aspects of Wisdom's privileges as my Right Hand Man and now no one had anything over him.

I decided not to buy lasagne. It had been Wisdom's favourite meal so I bought spaghetti bolognaise instead. Mdala would not have cared had I bought two bread rolls as long as it was a take-away.

During the meal, I asked Mdala why he and Wisdom had dressed the way they did for the court case.

"Because our friends who know about these things told us not to look smart. The police do not like that. The people in the courtroom do not like that. We black people must always know our place. It was also not good that Wisdom did not use an interpreter. You could see he was clever and that was not good. I am glad he has gone to save himself from more trouble. Haw, we miss Wisdom."

Fourteen

*T*wo weeks before my departure, Nigel phoned,

"Hi Roger, haven't seen you for a long time – circumstances and all that. Elaine and I would like to give you a farewell party at the Country Club. Are you in for it?"

"I appreciate your gesture and of course I accept. Thank you."

Without time to consider the pros and cons, I had accepted their invitation knowing that at its worst, it would be interesting. The date we set was for my last Saturday in the country.

In the meantime, Charles arrived at my flat unexpectedly one evening – dressed as before in a flat-boys uniform.

"Good morning my friend." he greeted me, "Condolences in an unhappy situation. You look well despite the harrowing time you've had."

"Good to see you Charles. I'm doing all right but I need time to regain some sort of normality in my life. I can do without this emotional stuff."

"I believe you. I hope we will both live to see the day that you can come back to a free and democratic South Africa, when you can visit me and I can visit you without fear of the consequences."

"I hope so too. Who knows? By the way, have you heard news of Wisdom? I feel anxious about him.

"No, but I think everything must have gone well. Bad news travels fast and we have not heard anything. Ugogo worries and I try to reassure her."

I gave Charles the money that I had kept in my safe for that purpose. At first, he was speechless. Then he thanked me profusely. I suggested that he put an amount in Ugogo's account and the rest he should use at his own discretion to benefit the community. Being able to give direct help to a worthy cause gave me a feeling of immense satisfaction.

We wished each other well and as I watched Charles leave, a wave of wistfulness washed over me. Everything I did, everyone I saw now was for the last time.

I decided to go away for a week to fill my empty days and chose to go to Umhlanga Rocks. I was more a mountain person but my frame of mind decided me that it would be unwise to go climbing.

The Oyster Box where I stayed was a perfect choice. It was one of the oldest and most historic of the hotels on the north coast having been built in 1869 though updated and modernised a few times since then. The hotel exuded old-world charm and dignity.

My en-suite accommodation overlooked the swimming pool, the beach and the sea. When I stepped out of my bedroom onto the lawn, I walked a few yards and was at the hotel swimming pool. The wide beach was some metres below and the landmark was a lighthouse that had been there for even longer than the hotel.

The sparkling pool held more appeal for me than did the beach. I swam numerous lengths every morning before breakfast and then sat at the pool and read the Natal Mercury. It was a cheerful newspaper and I wondered how long it would be before I could enjoy a newspaper quite like it again. It carried only good news. There were the excellent sporting results, the South

African girls had made a name for themselves by winning the women's doubles at Wimbledon and the Natal cricket team had beaten Eastern Province. There was the political news - Sir de Villiers Graaf, the leader of the United Party, was in Durban and was being greeted by enthusiastic crowds; he felt confident that his party would defeat the government in the coming general election. On the educational side, more students were progressing to university and other institutions of higher learning than ever before. The social page carried pictures of young people going overseas, those enjoying the horse races and there were pictures of socialites doing the giddy round of cocktail parties and dinner dances. The weather forecast predicted a continuation of the superb winter days. Yes, I enjoyed that paper and the short time it took to read it.

There was little to do in the evenings unless one went into Durban by way of the country road that meandered through the cane fields. I chose not to do that so I sat in the lounge and read or talked to people at the bar. I enjoyed going to bed at night because then I listened to the roar of the ocean; the waves crashing on the beach in a dramatic flaunting of nature's violence. Early in the morning, the tide went out and the water lapped gently around the rocks. Then the breakers came in. The sea along the Natal coast reflected my impression of South Africa, a country that was ruled by extremes and contrasts, beautiful but wild. A storm was never a little thunder and lightning. No, the thunder roared and the lightning was either sheet lighting that lit up the whole sky or fork lightning that was terrifying in its dangerous, stabbing intensity. When it rained, the rain poured down with ferocity. The people too were either tough because of the laws they made or they were tough because they had to endure those laws. The gentle ones struggled for survival. The undercurrents were like the tides of the Indian Ocean.

At the end of the week, I felt mentally and physically fit. I went back to my flat. Its emptiness and the significance thereof no longer bothered me. It was after all for a few more days only.

I had seen a few friends since my arrest but Nigel was not one of them. I could not blame him. He was a South African, straight as they come and he was not responsible for his ingrained bigotry. He evidently found it difficult to make allowances for anything I had done. On balance, it was great of him to consider giving me a farewell party let alone having the courage to do so. I had needed courage to accept knowing that at best people would regard me with puzzled incomprehension and some would search my face for signs of hitherto unnoticed, insalubrious characteristics.

I arrived to hear music wafting from the clubhouse, Louis Armstrong singing Mack the Knife, so that at least was a bright beginning to the evening. Nigel and Elaine met me at the door. They were relaxed and natural in their greeting and told me that I knew everyone.

There were about fifty guests and knowing Elaine's penchant for numbers and extravagance when it came to entertaining, I think they had invited many more people. Under the circumstances, they were probably well satisfied that the party had not been wholly boycotted. Those who turned up were good acquaintances of mine, if not friends, and there were a number of ex colleagues. It was an intimate and relaxed group of people and I considered the evening a perfect farewell to them and to South Africa.

I decided to make a short speech during the dinner.

"I would like to thank you both Nigel and Elaine for giving this personal and carefree evening in my honour – being carefree is something I have not experienced in recent times!" The guests laughed either in sympathy or in appreciation of the irony of my words and I continued, "thank you for giving me this opportunity to say goodbye to friends and I hope many of us will meet again. I regret that my stay in South Africa with all the fantastic experiences I have been privileged to be part of, has ended on a sour note but I leave this very beautiful country taking with me memories to last a lifetime." I raised my glass to drink a toast to them and was delighted when applause followed.

After dinner, the band played sedate dance music, waltzes and foxtrots, that sort of thing. Pleasant enough and it enabled those who were not dancing, to converse without the discomfort of raising their voices.

I asked Elaine for the first dance. She told me how upsetting the whole case had been for them. It had made her reassess her political ideas and she had come to believe that the Immorality Act was perhaps wrong after all, "but without it, our apartheid system would collapse."

"Yes, it would."

I changed the subject without expressing my opinion that that would be the first step in the right direction and said instead how much I appreciated their gesture in giving the party.

I danced with Barbara much of the evening. She reminisced about the end of year ball and how much fun it had been. I felt sorry for her and I hoped she would not waste her life thinking of what might have been. I encouraged her to look to the future and to forget unfulfilled hopes and dreams. When I had first met her, she gave the impression of being too serious for her age but she was a romantic at heart.

"Just consider all that *I* have to forget, Barbara! That said I have met many remarkable people, I have made a few genuine friends and I have enjoyed valuable experiences the memories of which will never fade. Those memories will more than compensate for the miseries of recent events. And I met a delightful person like you!"

Her eyes shone with tears and I immediately regretted saying that.

Barbara put her arms around me when we said goodbye, she could hardly talk but mumbled that she knew we would never see each other again. She would not have believed me had I said that she deserved better, someone who loved her in return. I hoped she would find that someone.

Alysha had not communicated with me from her clandestine address but I knew she would contact me when she considered the time right. I was impatient to speak to her again. I had missed her painfully and I wondered how she felt about the outcome of the trial. She would not have expected anything else. No one had been in doubt, not even before the trial began, as to what the eventual verdict would be. The only uncertainty was what the sentence would be. A "not guilty" verdict would have weakened the foundations of the Immorality Act.

Shortly before I left South Africa, a television company in London phoned me to make an appointment for a short interview on the day after my return to England. I agreed to cooperate though I had no idea what angle they wished to portray. I could rest assured on one thing; it would certainly not be pro apartheid!

It was late at night when my flight left Jan Smuts Airport. I hated leaving the country without Alysha particularly as I had no idea where she was. Most of my fellow passengers in first class were business people. No one gave any indication of recognising me and I was grateful for that.

My last view of Johannesburg with its millions of twinkling lights below was exquisite. The birds eye view of the city made me feel strangely detached from the reality of all that had happened. Goodbye South Africa and good luck with all your problems. You have been richly blessed with a great climate, scenic beauty, incomparable wildlife and natural resources. Adventurous people of different cultures and colours settled within your borders to make a better life for themselves. May they learn to appreciate each other and the rich diversity of the human race.

I thought of Wisdom and hoped that I would hear soon that he was safe. Charles had my address in England and had promised to write to me as soon as he had news of Wisdom.

In a matter of minutes, perhaps less, the plane left it all behind and suddenly there was nothing but darkness below. The adventure, the dream had ended and as with the ending of all fantasies, there was something infinitely sad about that.

Fifteen

The pilot made an early morning announcement,

"Good morning ladies and gentleman. Our scheduled time of arrival at Heathrow Airport is 0.800 hours local time. The weather in London is clear and fine. The temperature on the ground is 12 degrees. I hope you have enjoyed your flight and thank you for flying British Airways."

When I stepped off the plane, it was with tremendous relief to see that there was not a barrage of photographers waiting to meet me. I planned to spend two days in London in order to take part in the promised television interview and was pleased that I would be able to do so without advance publicity. The media in South Africa had invaded my personal privacy to the extent that I expected to be hounded by the press wherever I went. The queues at Customs and Immigration moved steadily. There was a sea of faces, hundreds of people waiting to meet arriving passengers. No one paid attention to me nor did I to them. I pushed my trolley passed the crowd towards the exit and suddenly felt someone's arms go around my waist from behind,

"Guess who?" she asked and I spun round to see Alysha! My heart leapt with joy as I looked at her in disbelief. I swung her off her feet, kissed and hugged her and held her close. Those moments, unexpected and fleeting as they were, were a marvellous, unforgettable encounter with ecstasy. We clung to each other lost for words.

"You have a lot of explaining to do my dear Alysha," I said at last wondering what she was doing there and how long she had been in England and then I remembered Boetie's advice. I loved her dearly so why not say it again!

"I've missed you so much Darling. Have you any idea how much I love you?"

"Only an idea - and I adore you! I could hardly wait to see you again. We must have some time together, just the two of us, so I've taken the liberty of making plans. We are going to drive to the hotel right now and I've booked for us to go to the Lake District until the weekend. I said I would confirm whether we will arrive tomorrow or the next day depending on any commitments you might have that I don't know about."

I told her about the interview planned for the next day so we could leave directly after that.

Sitting close to each other and holding hands in the back of a familiar London taxi, Alysha told me of the recent events in her life. I listened delighted and at the same time, I gave thanks that we were safe, that we no longer had to live a secret life, no need to worry about who might be spying on us from behind trees and doors, no longer scared to be seen in a car together. What did it matter that it was clear but chilly when we had our liberty and our right to choose? The exceptional climate and the splendours of South Africa melted into insignificance when compared with a country like Britain, a free and non-interventionist society.

"Give me this any day." I said out aloud

"What do you mean, 'give me this any day'?"

"Sorry, I was thinking aloud. I'll tell you later. I didn't mean to interrupt you so go on please."

"When I phoned your parents to tell them you were bearing up well during the court case, your mother invited me to escape from the intolerable situation I found myself in and to stay with them. Wasn't that kind of her! I did not hesitate and accepted her invitation immediately. Ma and Pitajee were relieved and so grateful to her. They had wanted me to go into hiding somewhere. But where could I go to? That was our dilemma."

"It sounds to me as though your visit was a great success."

"From my side, it was and I hope from Mum and Dad's too".

She was calling them Mum and Dad!

"Mum and I got on well from the first day and I have also got to know your brothers and sisters-in-law better though we haven't seen much of them. In our culture, when a woman marries she goes over to her husband's family so this is a normal situation for me. Of course, things have changed to a certain extent because many women are educated and have their own careers as I have."

"I'm so happy, Alysha."

The next morning Alysha said she would go to the studio with me. I did not think the interview would take more than fifteen minutes. Afterwards we would travel to Lake Windermere.

We arrived at the studio in good time and Alysha took a seat in the waiting room. My anticipated fifteen minutes stretched into the whole day! In the first place, I was introduced to the make-up artist. I thought my South African tan was adequate colour, but no, it was not. I hated every minute of being made up and covered in creams and powder and in the end the result was awful. An assistant showed me through to the studio where the interview was to take place.

"I wonder if you would mind telling my companion in the waiting room, that this is all taking much longer than I had expected. Do you by any chance have a cafeteria where she can wait?

"Leave it to me."

Camera operators put me in the correct position for the interview, they adjusted the lighting and then the interviewer arrived.

The person I called the assistant came back and whispered something to the director. He looked positively delighted at what he heard.

"Mr. Sinclair is the young lady in the waiting room perhaps Miss Patel who was the mystery person in the recent drama in South Africa?"

"That's her."

"This is most exciting. Do you think she would agree to being interviewed alongside you? That would appeal to a wide public. Our job is to attract a large number of viewers to the programme and since there was a great deal of interest and sympathy for you both during the court case, we wish to take advantage of that and strike while the iron is hot. Anti apartheid sympathies were aroused and we want to help that cause wherever and however we can."

"I cannot speak for Miss Patel but I shall ask her."

"Do your best. She will make all the difference to the programme."

When I told Alysha of the suggestion that she too be interviewed, she agreed instantly.

"Of course I'll do it; anything to let the world see the misery our regime causes to all levels of society, let alone to us personally."

I watched the Director's face when I introduced him to Alysha. He was taken aback at first and then he recovered his self-possession and was charged with renewed enthusiasm. He knew instantly that she would be an asset in any film. She would be the star of this one.

"Shouldn't I also be made up for the cameras?" Alysha asked the director.

"No, sweetheart, you are perfect as you are. It's the pale faces we have to work on."

I winked at Alysha. I had not considered myself a pale face.

Suddenly, nothing was good enough. Flowers had to be placed on a table to supplement the austere background. He told the operators responsible for the lighting to soften the harsh, bright lights usually used for serious interviews and he ordered that two less formal and more comfortable chairs be brought from an adjoining studio. When he was satisfied with the ambiance, he asked us whether we would like to go through the questions that were likely to be asked of us. Neither Alysha nor I wanted that as we knew we could cope with whatever questions were thrown at us and we envisaged a discussion rather than a questions and answer routine.

Surprisingly, neither of us was nervous when the cameras rolled. We mentioned afterwards that we had thoroughly enjoyed exposing the South African government for what it was. The director was in raptures, he being the melodramatic type. His pronouncement at the end of the long session was that it would be a rip-roaring success! Did we have any objections to him censoring the interview where he thought it necessary?

"No, none at all." To be honest, we did not much care what he did with it.

"The programme will be screened at 8.30 pm immediately after the news on Tuesday of next week. That gives us time for it to be publicised in advance, edit it and get it into shipshape order. Thank you to both of you. I am personally most grateful to you." He looked only at Alysha when he spoke.

We shook hands with the director and left. Because it was getting late, we spent another night in town and left for the Lake District the next morning.

The Lake District worked wonders. Driving down to Devon four days later with Alysha at my side, I felt carefree as I had not been in a very long time. I looked forward to seeing my family again and to settling down to a normal life. The future would take care of itself.

When we arrived home, Mum came running out tears streaming down her cheeks and she hugged me as though she had hardly expected to see me again. Dad put his arm around my shoulders and we walked indoors. My brothers and their wives were at the house as were my nephews and nieces so there was much happy laughter and fun. Dad popped a bottle of champagne and Alysha handed round her homemade samooses. Mum took me aside and said confidentially in the manner of someone who has made a surprising discovery,

"I've got to know Alysha and she is like the daughter I never had. Both Dad and I love her. She has taught me to make delicious Indian curry dishes and she genuinely appreciates my cooking!"

"I'm so pleased, Mum, that means a lot to me." Then Dad called out,

"Oh, by the way, Roger, there's a letter for you on my desk. Don't let me forget to give it to you."

"I'll get it now if you don't mind. It may be important."

It was from Charles!

I went to my bedroom where my suitcase was still unpacked, sat on my bed and opened the letter.

My dear Friend,

I am very sorry to be the bearer of bad news but there is no other way so I shall be blunt. Wisdom is dead.

We heard yesterday that he made it to Mozambique. He was very ill when he got there. His guides took him to a mission hospital where nuns cared for him with skill and kindness but they could not save him. The doctor said he had developed inflammation of the brain resulting from a severe blow to his head. It must have been at the time of his violent interrogation at the hands of the police shortly before the trial began. He never felt well after that.

From the time Wisdom was admitted to hospital until he died, comrades took it in turns to be with him and held his hand throughout. That comforted him. They knew that by the occasional pressure of his hand. Before he died, Wisdom managed to say, in Zulu of course, that he loved Ugogo and did not want her to grieve for long because he was happy. They said his eyes glazed over and he looked into space. Then he said in English, "Tell Sir Sink..." His message was garbled and he must have realised that because he tried again, "Tell Sir..." Those were his last words then he closed his eyes and passed away peacefully. I feel it is important for you to know that his thoughts were with you at the end.

We have no further news.

"Sala Kahle".

Charles.

Skivvy, my Right Hand Man - dead? It would not sink into my befuddled brain. What was wrong with me, why wouldn't it sink in? *Skivvy was dead!*

I thought of his youthful, worried expression, his concerns for the children he hoped to have one day, I remembered how he had enjoyed our take-aways when he proudly ate the 'European way,' how he had loved his title, Right Hand Man - and his uniforms! I put my head down fighting tears unsuccessfully, fighting for composure.

I pulled myself together but could not face going back to the drawing room just yet. Alysha came in and I handed her the letter. She had never met Wisdom but she felt as though she knew him. Alysha read the letter in silence, put her arm around my shoulders, kissed me and then left the room. She must have told the family because the cheerful atmosphere had taken on a sombre mood when I put my head round the door and said I would be going for a long walk on my own.

When I got to the beach, I took off my shoes and socks, rolled up my trouser legs and walked along the waters edge for about an hour. The air was salty, the wind blew around my head and the water was cold and turbulent, exactly as I felt.

I was on the verge of depression. How easy it would be to give into it – and how pleasant! I would not do so. My example would always be the strength and character of the black people whom I had met in South Africa and whose courage I admired.

Poor Ugogo, hers was the greatest loss of all.

On Tuesday evening, my parents and Alysha sat glued to the television for the transmission of "our" programme. I did not have the heart for it and said they could tell me about it afterwards. I never wanted to see it however good or bad it was.

When it was over, they were thrilled with the content and the production. Their consensus was that it was excellent. It must have been! If Max and the anti-apartheid movement had hoped for wide publicity through the case against me, they had reason to cheer. The interview was in demand by television networks abroad and was made available to an international audience.

Offers flooded in for Alysha not only from English and American filmmakers but also from Indian producers. That was an ego-boost and exciting for her but she said she did not intend to swap her career as a physicist for stardom. I was relieved to hear it. I hoped she would swap everything for the role of wife and, hopefully in time, motherhood.

I was most fortunate too because instead of film offers, I received job offers. The most attractive was from the Kennedy Space Centre. The introduction to our interview had been one of glowing praise regarding both Alysha and my academic backgrounds. No prospective employer could take that at face value so the Director asked me to forward my curriculum vitae.

At last, I could get excited about something. Alysha and I had flirted with the idea of immigrating to the United States but with all the drama, we had not had time to think seriously about it or to apply for jobs or permits. Now this unforeseen opportunity!

I could not think of a more challenging or fascinating job than one in the newest and most ambitious of all programmes, that of space exploration.

"Alysha, I have an exciting job offer to work at the Kennedy Space Centre. How do you feel about it? This could be exactly what we have been hoping to find; a country that will accept us without colour discrimination, where we will feel at home and make it our home and one with prospects for the future!"

"I would love it! First, I have to go back to South Africa to work through my three months notice at the university. Ma and Pitajee want me home and when I'm back in South Africa, I will discuss wedding plans with them. They are sure to take over in the traditional Indian manner even if that's the only traditional thing about our wedding!" Alysha was over the moon.

A week later, Alysha went back to South Africa and I flew to the United States for the interview. At the end of it, the Director made me a firm offer that I accepted without hesitation. I was thrilled about the development work involved and the challenging opportunities.

"Will you be available to start work with us in three weeks time, on the first of next month; the sooner the better from our point of view?"

I mentioned that I would need a fortnight's leave during the next few months since Alysha and I planned to get married. He congratulated me and said that would be no problem.

We shook hands – as quickly as that, a done deal. That was America for you.

I stayed for a few extra days to look into the housing market and then decided to rent a condominium for six months. That would give Alysha and me time to make up our minds about buying a house. Together we would decide where it should be located and how big it should be. We hoped to have children without having to move house again. In the meantime, I had to live somewhere.

Sixteen

Orlando, Florida, was to be our hometown. Washington or New York may have been more exciting but I was in high spirits at the prospect of settling in Florida. The climate would suit Alysha perfectly since, like her hometown Durban in Natal, it was subtropical. There were numerous tourist attractions in the area and those would keep us busy while we were finding our feet in our new environment.

We expected that we would experience a culture shock although I had been prepared for a few American idiosyncrasies. Friends who had lived there said that as a nation they were friendly but superficial. They were well versed in pleasantries, "Have a nice day", "You must come and visit us," "How lucky we are that you have come to visit us!" Even waiters in restaurants automatically used Christian names when addressing senior citizens. "Good evening, my name is Joe. I will be your waiter this evening. What are your names?" He did not expect to hear "Mr. and Mrs. Anything" not even from eighty year olds!

Alysha was delighted to hear that I had found a condominium and she said that Ma and Pitajee were actively occupied with our wedding plans. They had graciously accepted that I was to be their son-in-law instead of what they had always hoped for, a suitable, well-educated Indian of their choice. "They took you to their hearts when you spoke so bravely and so candidly during the trial," she wrote.

Alysha wrote that Ma and Pitajee hoped to arrange our wedding in Acapulco. "They are working on it." Acapulco, she said, rested between the Sierra Madre del Sur Mountains and the Acapulco Bay and had twenty miles of beach.

She asked whether 18th April would suit me and suggested that I send them a list of the guests I would like to invite along with their addresses. She added that it was going to be a surprise from beginning to end!

I knew that my parents, my brothers and their families and perhaps a few other extended family members and possibly a few good friends would attend but I couldn't imagine that many people would travel to Mexico for my wedding.

Apparently, getting visas and conforming to all the legal requirements for a wedding in the United States was proving to be a headache so they had chosen an easier and more romantic destination. Mr. Patel had business friends in Mexico and they were lending a helping hand and making valuable suggestions. He had flown over to approve of the tentative arrangements they had made and to finalise bookings. I was pleased that Mr. and Mrs. Patel were involved in planning our wedding that was so different from anything they had ever had in mind for their daughter. As far as I was concerned, the wedding could take place anywhere on earth as long as it finally happened.

My only responsibility was to have a cream coloured suit tailor made with thick silk lapels and a cummerbund of the same thick silk. Illustrations accompanied the design for the suit as they did for the collarless shirt that was a necessary part of the outfit. Apparently, I would be required to wear that for the wedding ceremony. I attended to my only task immediately.

While Alysha a great distance away, concentrated on our wedding, I settled into my challenging new job with enthusiasm. From the first day, I met incredibly interesting and highly talented colleagues and felt privileged to be on the same team with them.

The work was demanding of my best efforts in the field of physics and mathematics and I was absorbed in it. I was pleased that Alysha and her parents wanted to take over all the wedding plans so that all I had to do was be there on time.

On the 17th April, I flew to Acapulco. Mr. and Mrs. Patel met me at the airport,

"Hello Roger, wonderful to see you again." We embraced each other.

On the way to the hotel, Mr. Patel told me of the plans for the rest of the day.

"Your parents and family members will be arriving this afternoon. We will welcome them at the airport and bring them to the hotel. You might want to go yourself but it is our tradition that the bride's family welcomes the bridegroom's family to the wedding festivities. In the meantime, we will now take you to your hotel. The plan is that a driver will call for you at eight o'clock this evening and then you will fetch Alysha. You will both be taken to a restaurant together where all our overseas guests will be waiting to greet you and where we will have dinner together."

"Surely I can see Alysha before then?"

"No, you will see her in her first bridal gown and not any sooner." They laughed at my impatience.

The driver called for me at 8 o'clock sharp and then we went to a nearby hotel to fetch Alysha. I went inside and there she was gorgeous in an elaborate red sari. An artist friend of Alysha's had painted her hands and feet hands with henna. The designs were fine and intricate. She told me that it had taken eight hours to complete and during that time, her sisters-in-law had entertained her with songs and stories. I hadn't seen her for so long and yet I dared not take her in my arms for fear of ruining her outfit or her make-up or anything else that had been so meticulously arranged. I didn't dare even kiss her hand because of the paint!

"You look wonderful, Darling, and though I want to kiss you, I will resist until later but in the meantime you are a dream and *I love you!*"

The chauffeur drove us to a superb restaurant that Mr. and Mrs. Patel had rented for the night. It was surrounded by a panoramic view of Acapulco Bay as seen from the Cliffs and the lights twinkled in the distance. It was a most romantic scene. The restaurant was in semi-darkness when we arrived. As we approached the door, the lights went on; a band struck up and everyone raised their champagne glasses and sang a song that friends had composed especially for us.

Our parents and all our family members lined up to greet us. I had not met Alysha's two brothers and their wives before so after our parents, they were next in line. Many people had come over from South Africa. Amongst them were Mira and Goofy. It was good to see them again. Then to my delighted surprise Boetie, Annabel and their three daughters were amongst the guests. I could hardly believe my eyes when having greeted them, I saw Charles Mkhize step forward. Perhaps because of the apparent impossibility of his presence and because of my special association with him, he was the most fantastic surprise of all.

"Charles, you are the last person I could have expected to see in Mexico on my wedding day! What a wonderful surprise but then I could never have expected to be in Mexico myself on my wedding day!"

"Can you imagine *my* surprise when Mr. Patel contacted me with an invitation to come to your wedding in Mexico, all expenses paid and a week's holiday? It was enough to give me a heart attack! I could not believe it, me, Charles Mkhize, schoolmaster from a tiny, rural village in Zululand. Mr. Patel arranged everything for me including my passport. That was a miracle. I would not have known where to begin or how to go about it. It is the most difficult thing in the world for a black person to get a passport to leave the country. I know of no one who has succeeded. In my position, no black man would even try."

"Charles, I cannot imagine how he did it but am I pleased he did! I am delighted that we will have time to talk at length during the coming days. I hope you have a pleasant evening. Is anyone taking care of you?"

"Annabel and Boetie have included me from the moment we met in the Departures lounge at Jan Smuts."

"You couldn't be in better company."

Alysha and I then circulated amongst our other guests each one a treat to see.

If my father-in-law had asked me to compose my dream list of guests, this would have been it exactly. No wonder Alysha had said that our wedding would be a surprise from beginning to end.

The ceremony the next day was a Hindu service adapted to the circumstances. It took place in a large tent erected on the beach and filled with a variety of colourful, tropical flowers. Alysha wore a different red sari. This one was heavily embroidered with gold thread and she wore the most exquisite gold jewellery including bracelets and earrings. She wore a hand-crafted gold ornament in the middle of her hairline on her forehead. Her sandals showed off her dainty, meticulously-painted feet. My bride was an exotic Asian beauty with a kind and gentle nature and I hoped she would always be happy with me an ordinary Englishman with no pretence at being anything else, as dull as they come by comparison.

There were more guests at the reception than had attended the dinner the evening before and many were business associates of Mr. Patel and friends who lived in Mexico.

A Hindu priest, also from Reservoir Hills, South Africa, presided over the wedding that began with garlands being placed around our necks. Alysha than applied sandalwood paste to my forehead and I made a round red mark on her forehead that should stay there for as long as we were married. I wondered about that!

The priest lit a small fire and we had to walk around it seven times. Alysha led the way for the first three rounds and then she followed me for the remaining four rounds.

All were long established rituals with symbolic meaning. As in a Christian wedding service, we had to make certain promises:

to earn a living for our family and respect their abundance,
to live a healthy lifestyle for each other,
to be concerned for the partner's welfare, happiness and friendship
throughout our religious-centred lives,
to eat and drink together and be with each other on special occasions,
to desire children for whom we would be responsible and love,
to adapt to the other person at any given time and place.

Then I, the bridegroom had to recite the traditional prayer to the bride including,

"I am the words and you are the melody, I am the melody and you are the words."

The service was unfamiliar to me but I did not find it strange.

I placed my gift, a gold necklace studded with small diamonds, around Alysha's neck. Then my father put a wedding necklace consisting of a gold chain with gold semicircles and black onyx stones, a gift from both families, around his daughter-in-laws neck and that symbolised the union of our two families. Gold rings on her toes symbolised that we were married.

Alysha whispered that she loved me. I took her hand and kissed it.

Our honeymoon was unconventional, at least from a European point of view. Instead of our going away together, it was a time of family togetherness with friends. Mr. Patel had invited all the overseas family and friends to stay for a week as his guests. We were grateful to him for that. It would have been disappointing to see dear friends who had travelled half way round the world to attend our wedding and not have time to talk to them.

Alysha and I were in a different hotel from the guests otherwise we shared our time with them sightseeing, enjoying the beach and its attractions, the swimming pool and nightclubbing with those who so wished. I was particularly pleased to have long discussions with Charles and with Boetie and his family and of course with Goofy and Mira too. I had not seen Goofy and Mira since the night of my arrest. How ludicrous it seemed to me then and always thereafter that I could not have contact with my friends without running the risk of breaking the conditions of my suspended sentence.

When I asked Charles about Ugogo, he said that Wisdom had been the centre of her world but she was bearing up bravely. She kept herself busy and helped with the youngest children at school.

Charles said that she was looking forward to his return, as was everyone else in the village and to hearing about his trip and the wedding. The villagers had been almost as excited as he was so he was particularly pleased that Mr. Patel had promised to give him a selection of photographs that he could show to the people when he got back. Charles added that the trip was far more than a dream come true because in his wildest dreams, he could never have imagined anything like it! Then he told me of a different aspect to the exciting experience,

"One of the most significant impressions and surprises of this trip has been seeing the tremendous inequality in living standards in Acapulco. In contrast to the glitz and glamour and the unimaginable affluence of the rich, are the slums where there is obviously dire poverty. The slums are on the slopes of the mountain. I had not expected to see anything like KwaMashu outside the borders of Africa!"

Ours was a wedding that brought together South African friends of different cultural backgrounds, Asian, white and black in harmony and in celebration. They learned to know and appreciate each other and share their impressions of a part of the world new to all of them. If the country could ever emulate that in the future, it would be taking a big step towards the ending of apartheid and fulfilling its potential as a paradise for all. Until then, I would not be able to go back to South Africa.

Seventeen

$\mathcal{M}$any years have passed since our wedding. The theme of Pitajee's speech at our reception was "Marriage is the beginning and not the end" so it seems appropriate that my story ends not there but here.

Alysha and I are grateful to America for taking us in and making us feel at home, for giving us a place to live in peace and safety and without prejudice. Alysha stopped wearing her sari except on special occasions and to special events so that she would fit in better with Americans. She went to a leading beauty salon where Geoffrey, highly regarded in the community for his expertise, cut and styled her hair in the latest fashion and she even took to wearing jeans and sneakers.

Do we feel American? No but we are extremely happy living here. Our non-identical twin sons, Sanjay and Rajiv, belong nowhere else. They are proud to be Americans and have no wish to have dual nationality. By birth, in loyalty and in deed, they are Americans. They are sporty fellows and in that, they take after my father and my brothers. They inherited their mother's black hair, her brown, almond-shaped eyes and Indian features. They ended up my height and with my build. Their honey-coloured skin is purely their own, being unique in both our families. They are good-looking boys - at least we, and the girls, think so.

During the course of time, we made friends in America usually through my work and through our sons and their friends. Alysha established contact with our first friends, Geeta and Roy Chandra.

Soon after we settled in Orlando, Alysha decided to try out the local manicure/pedicure centre. In the beginning, she was trying out everything! The assistants were all well trained personnel from Vietnam and Alysha noticed that amongst their clients were a number of international women. While her feet were soaking in a luxurious footbath, Alysha observed those around her and saw that the person sitting opposite was a young Indian woman. She had a pleasant, friendly face so Alysha decided to speak to her.

"I would like to introduce myself. My name is Alysha Sinclair. I am from South Africa and my husband is British. We are new arrivals in the United States."

"I am pleased to meet you. My name is Geeta Chandra. My husband has recently completed three years as a gynaecologist at the Mayo Clinic and has joined a practise in Orlando so we too are new to this part of the country. We are both from Bombay."

That was how a long and highly valued friendship began.

Roy took care of Alysha during her pregnancy and delivered our sons. He saved her life that hung precariously in the balance for two agonising days. He advised us that she should have no more children so we were doubly grateful that we had two healthy babies.

My work in helping to get shuttles into space is so fascinating that I could work day and night and never feel that it is too long or too much! It is interesting to meet astronauts and to live through their exciting travels in space knowing that their safety and their successes depend on a whole team on the ground. I am only a small spoke in the wheel but to be involved at all is exciting and more rewarding than any other job I could possibly envisage.

With the benefit of hindsight, I can thank the court case in South Africa for the path my life followed. It opened the way to an internationally broadcasted television interview that in turn led to this particular job offer. There must be some truth in the saying, "Every cloud has a silver lining!"

Alysha and I look back on a wonderful life together with its joys and its inevitable sorrows. We are most grateful for the families we were born into, the one we produced and the friends we made along the way. Many of those dear to us have passed away.

Ma and Pitajee could not have been more gracious and generous parents-in-law. Having done their best to discourage Alysha from marrying me in the first place, they accepted the inevitable good-naturedly and our families integrated in friendship and affection in the true Hindu tradition. From the day we got married, they never called me Roger I was always "Son."

My mother adored Alysha and the feeling was mutual. We still make annual trips to England so that we can keep in touch with close family members and with my British heritage for the benefit of our sons. We always enjoy being in London for a few days to see the West End shows and for Alysha to shop in her favourite shop, Harrods, before we travel along the narrow, winding, hedgerows to our destination in Devon.

Boetie and Annabel were regular visitors to our home in Florida. We welcomed their visits with happy anticipation and we were all sorry when the time came for them to leave again.

A week after their last visit to us, Boetie went to Cape Town to open an art exhibition. The exhibition was a great success with the media present, the public jostling to meet him and sales hectic. Afterwards, on his way back to his hotel, he was involved in a collision with a drunken driver and was very seriously injured. Annabel phoned to tell us the shocking news that Boetie was in a coma. I wanted to fly out to them immediately and Alysha agreed that I should do so. Unfortunately, the South African Embassy in Washington stymied those plans when they refused to consider my application for an emergency visa, not even on compassionate grounds. The next devastating message from Annabel was that Boetie had passed away without regaining consciousness.

I wrestled with the shocking news that my best friend had gone for good. I remembered the words quoted at funerals, "in the midst of life we are in death." I supposed it meant that death is part of life but there was no comfort in that. The fact remained that Boetie's death was helluva ruddy heartbreaking and blerrie difficult to accept.

Alysha kept in close touch with Annabel and tried to comfort her but she was inconsolable. Our much-loved friend could not live on her own in Nottingham Road because it would have been far too dangerous. Overwhelmed with grief, she was faced with having to sell their beloved home that had rung with laughter and fun and where they had shared true and enduring love that included their three cherished daughters.

Annabel wrote that Boetie's family were deeply distressed that there had been such a long estrangement and that they had not seen their brother in years. In their sorrow, they realised how petty were the prejudices that came between family members. They regretted taking life for granted as though it would never change, would never end.

Annabel went back to England with Pauline. Her two eldest daughters, Darlene and Charlene, immigrated to Australia with their young families. The most recent news from Annabel was that she and Pauline could not settle in England and they too were planning to go to Perth, Australia.

Boetie's masterpiece, the incomparable painting of Wisdom and the kraal scene hangs in the drawing room where it has been since the day we moved into our home in Florida. When I gaze at it in wonderment as I often do, I am transported back in time to long ago. Memories of special people and exceptional experiences in a far-off land fill me with deep and abiding gratitude. They enriched my life forever.

THE AUTHOR

Helen J. Anderson, author of "The Sun Kept Shining" was born in Durban, South Africa. After completing her formal education at the Durban Business College, she lived in Salisbury, Rhodesia (later Harare, Zimbabwe) where she met her husband.

The Federation of Rhodesia and Nyasaland was dissolved in 1966 and the family moved from Salisbury to Lusaka, capital of the newly independent country, Zambia, and lived there for five years.

Nine years after transferring to South Africa, Helen and her husband moved with their family to The Netherlands where they now live.